THE RELUCTANT JOURNEY
of DAVID CONNORS

A Novel

THE RELUCTANT JOURNEY
of DAVID CONNORS

DON LOCKE

OUR GUARANTEE TO YOU

We believe so strongly in the message of our books that we are making this quality guarantee to you. If for any reason you are disappointed with the content of this book, return the title page to us with your name and address and we will refund to you the list price of the book. To help us serve you better, please briefly describe why you were disappointed. Mail your refund request to: NavPress, P.O. Box 35002, Colorado Springs, CO 80935.

NavPress
P.O. Box 35001
Colorado Springs, Colorado 80935

ISBN-13: 978-1-60006-152-3
ISBN-10: 1-60006-152-4

Cover design by The DesignWorks Group, Charles Brock, www.thedesignworksgroup.com
Cover photo by Pixelworks Studio, Steve Gardner
Author photo by Michael Christman

Creative Team: Jeff Gerke, Jamie Chavez, Reagen Reed, Arvid Wallen, Pat Reinheimer, Kathy Guist

This novel is a work of fiction. Names, characters, places, and incidents are either the product of the author's imagination or are used fictitiously. Any resemblance to actual events, locales, organizations, or persons, living or dead, is entirely coincidental and beyond the intent of either the author or publisher.

Unless otherwise identified, all Scripture quotations in this publication are taken from the *Revised Standard Version Bible* (RSV), copyright 1946, 1952, 1971, by the Division of Christian Education of the National Council of the Churches of Christ in the USA, used by permission, all rights reserved. Other versions used include the HOLY BIBLE: NEW INTERNATIONAL VERSION® (NIV®), Copyright © 1973, 1978, 1984 by International Bible Society, used by permission of Zondervan Publishing House, all rights reserved; and the *New King James Version* (NKJV). Copyright © 1982 by Thomas Nelson, Inc. Used by permission. All rights reserved.

Published in association with Jill Grosjean, Jill Grosjean Literary Agency

Locke, Don, 1949-
    The reluctant journey of David Connors : a novel / Don Locke.
       p. cm.
    ISBN-13: 978-1-60006-152-3
    ISBN-10: 1-60006-152-4
    1. Forgiveness--Fiction. 2. Self-realization--Fiction. 3. Christmas
stories. I. Title.
PS3612.O248R45 2007
813'.6--dc22

                                    2007015857

Printed in the United States of America

1 2 3 4 5 6 7 8 9 10 / 10 09 08 07

FOR A FREE CATALOG OF NAVPRESS BOOKS & BIBLE STUDIES,
CALL 1-800-366-7788 (USA) OR 1-800-839-4769 (CANADA).

For Rick and Mar,
for their love and support from day one

Every good endowment and every perfect gift is from above,
coming down from the Father of lights
with whom there is no variation or shadow due to change.

JAMES 1:17

CONTENTS

one

THE MYSTERIOUS DEATH OF AUNT LOUISE

For me feelings have always been a bit like wading in a swamp late at night: You wouldn't want to spend too much time there for fear of eventually encountering something really unpleasant. But sometimes those murky waters just have a way of rising up around you all on their own.

That's exactly what happened that winter night as I sat behind the wheel of my brand-new 1995 Volvo parked in front of my family's house. My body wouldn't stop trembling, and my eyes couldn't stop staring at the beautifully decorated Christmas tree framed in the bay window, the colorful lights flashing on and off.

It wasn't only Kathy's carefully chosen words, whispered to me several minutes earlier in the living room, that sent me into the grip of this panic attack:

"David, this trial separation . . . it's not working out."

"What do you mean?"

"I'm not sure what I expected from it. I guess I was hoping . . ."

"What?"

"I was hoping that I'd miss you."

It felt like she'd pulled the plug on me. The words sounded cruel, but I knew hurting me wasn't her intention; she was just being honest. It was Kathy's sincerity and candor that first attracted me to her fifteen years earlier—aside from her obvious beauty and charm.

No, equally responsible for this whirlpool of dread was the look on our son's face. I'd scooped Jeremy's limp body off the living room floor when I first arrived; at nine years old he was nearly too heavy to be cradled in my arms.

"Jeremy was so sure you'd be showing up any second," Kathy said. She'd already put our daughter, Kelly, to bed.

As I carried him off in his red pajamas to his bedroom, his body began to stiffen and stir. I could see his eyes barely opening in the dark. "Where were you, Dad? Did you see the tree?"

"It looks great, Jer. Go back to sleep, okay?" I laid him down in his bed, looked into those sleepy eyes, and watched it finally happen. "You said you'd be here, Dad. You promised." His last remaining spark of faith in me dimmed, then went out. I secured his stuffed dog, Albert, under his arm and pulled the blankets up around his small shoulders. As I kissed him goodnight, something about it felt so final.

When I returned to the living room, Kathy was sitting cross-legged in our old rocker. As I sat down on the couch across from her, Morgan, our golden retriever, jumped up next to me and laid his head on my lap. Kathy slowly leaned back and forth, setting the chair in motion, staring at the tree. I wanted to remind her that as the owner and artistic director of the computer games software company that provided for all of us, I had a certain obligation to make an appearance at the employee holiday party. I wanted to explain that the unexpected snowstorm had left the tollway backed up, and that, once again, *it wasn't my fault*. But even I had grown tired of my excuses. So I just listened as Kathy spoke calmly—too calmly—about my failings as a father, my inadequacies as a husband. She said she'd always sensed a space between us, a gap that she had always hoped would eventually close.

"Kathy . . . I want to come home."

"Why? Even when you did live here, David, you were a ghost. I spent the last dozen years trying to get your attention. It didn't matter if we were in a conversation at the dinner table or in bed making love. A part of you was always off in another dimension."

I wanted her to get mad—to blister me like she had in the past. But her analytical words sounded more like a woman who'd finally given up.

A large silver ornament broke loose from an upper branch and tumbled down through the Christmas tree, coming to rest unbroken on the white linen cloth around the base. Kathy remained focused on us.

"I don't think that we were ever truly intimate," she said. "Maybe only in my imagination. There was a time when I thought I had the power to make that intimacy real. I thought all I had to do was just to try harder, be a better wife . . . pray a little more. Why didn't you tell me back then that I'd always be dealing with a ghost?"

I pleaded the only defense I knew—professing my love for her one last time. She responded with a kindness and sympathy in her green eyes that defied her words. "I'm not sure you know what love is, David."

My impulse was to dig in my heels, but denying her accusation wouldn't have made it any less true. Still, I wanted to fix us—to turn a dial, flip a switch. Maybe most of all I wanted to cry. But my tears wouldn't flow. Kathy had no such problem, and she fled the room, bawling, leaving me alone with my miserable thoughts.

I didn't want to leave. I looked around the room at our history: the rocking chair I bought for Kathy just before Jeremy was born . . . the broken antique clock that I'd always meant to fix . . . the framed photo of the four of us taken during our vacation in Yellowstone, Old Faithful erupting behind us. I remembered how brave Jeremy was to ask a stranger if he would take our picture. And I remembered the old man's words as he handed the camera back to me: "You're a lucky man."

As I stood up to leave, I picked up the fallen ornament, the fish-eyed distortion of my own face staring back at me. I gently hung it on a branch, gave Morgan a pat on the head, and walked out the door.

Sitting behind the wheel, I turned the key in the ignition and felt as if I'd died inside. Now my irresponsibility and my alienation had finally awakened a demon that first yawned, then stretched itself and slowly rose up from this dead place inside me to stake its claim, wrapping itself around my heart with a sadness and despair that registered off the charts of my experience.

The blue radio light on the dash blinked, and from the speakers came the voice of a man desperate to sell radial tires. I poked several station buttons in hopes of replacing him with a song—preferably an old song, one that could send me decades away from there. But Karen Carpenter's lush, unmistakable voice crooning "Merry Christmas, Darling" only made me think of anorexia nervosa . . . and Christmas without my family.

Snow crunched beneath my wheels as I glanced one last time at the Christmas tree in the window and saw the lights go out completely. There were no melodies capable of lifting this weight from me, so I shut the radio off, leaving myself with only Kathy's words repeating over and over in my head. I drove between the rows of snowplowed drifts that marked suburban property lines, and continued through the forest preserve–turned–wonderland, trying to outrun myself.

Without any real destination in mind, I merged onto the Edens Expressway, where traffic was as light and well spaced as the falling snow. The growing Chicago skyline slowly glided back and forth in front of me, the city lights drawing me in like a hypnotist's crystal. I was barely aware of the approaching exit for my apartment complex.

After Kathy had decided it was best for us to separate, I searched dozens of apartments looking for a place that I'd find sufficiently deplorable—one that I hated so much that it could never feel like home to me. Finally I located the ideal place. I found its avocado green walls and ocher shag carpeting impressively repulsive, the mold creeping along the bathroom tiles despicable. But it was the unmistakable, repugnant fragrance of aged cat urine lingering in the air that sealed the deal for me. I despised the place. It was perfect.

The small, lifeless dwelling had served as my deserted island while I waited those three long months to be rescued, but now with the search officially called off, the thought of going back to the apartment that night to make it my permanent home was inconceivable. I sailed past the exit without giving it so much as a glance.

Minutes later I left the expressway behind and rolled through Old Town, slowing down in front of the kelly green neon leprechaun perched over the doorway to O'Malley's Pub. The second stool from the rear had become a refuge for me of late, but this feeling had grown bigger than any bar could hold. I eased my foot down on the accelerator.

Several blocks later I pulled up in front of the skyscraper where I worked, slid into a no-parking zone, and stepped out of my car and into the slush. Parading on the sidewalk in front of the forty-story skyscraper was an assortment of bodies shrinking beneath their winter coats, faces hiding behind woolen scarves, arms stretched by the weight of shopping bags. Some, no doubt, would be going home to empty houses, to fall asleep alone and to wake alone. I wondered how they did it — how they convinced their hearts not to care.

A young, rosy-cheeked Salvation Army worker was standing there on the sidewalk beside her red bucket, giving her bell a workout. I'd noticed her several times in the past week, and we'd never exchanged a look or a word. But that night, as I passed the girl, I heard her say, "Peace be with you, sir." Ignoring her, I continued on into the building.

With the rhythm of my tennis shoes squeaking on the marble floor, I entered the deserted lobby, and tunnel-visioned past Ernie, the night guard. "Burning the midnight oil, eh, Mr. Connors?" he called behind me.

Sleepwalking into a vacant elevator, I punched 39 and leaned back against the wall; the humming ride was nonstop and over in a moment. I gathered myself and stepped out onto our company's floor. Normally several animators and programmers would be working late, but with it being the holiday season, there wasn't a sign of life.

I flipped on an overhead set of lights and made my way over to my office, unlocked the door, and went in. A pile of sketches fluttered to the floor as I walked around my desk, but I ignored them. Sitting down in front of my computer, I dumped a key out of a crudely molded, colorful coffee cup that Jeremy made for me. I unlocked the bottom drawer. It glided opened, and I lifted out a small stack of *Sports Illustrated*, uncovering a nearly full fifth of Jack Daniels. I grabbed the bottle, twisted off the cap, and took a substantial swig.

Our marriage counselor had suggested more than once that I drank out of fear—to avoid my feelings. She'd frequently point her bony finger in my direction and say, "You, sir, need to get in touch with your feelings"—like it was just a matter of picking up the phone and calling Aunt Louise or something. The fact was "Aunt Louise" had been buried long ago, having died of some undisclosed disease.

Holding tight to the bottle, I maneuvered through the maze of mauve cubicles, down the hallway, and through the green door leading to the stairwell. As I climbed toward the rooftop, the muffled beats of my heart pounded in my ears, and I paused periodically to take a shot of whiskey.

I leaned my hip against the heavy access door and nudged it open. Stumbling onto the rooftop, I stepped into the light shining down from above the closing door. An undulating buzz emanating from the fixture sounded like something out of Frankenstein—the mad doctor pulling a switch to zap his creation with electrical current, jump-starting its new life. I raised my arms away from my sides, imagining the electrical charge of that buzz surging through my body, giving me new life.

I marched through the glistening, foot-deep powder, stopping short of the ledge. I closed my eyes, poured one last dose of medicine down my throat, and dropped the partly empty bottle at my side. With two long, mechanical strides, I reached the edge of the roof. I swept the snow off the ledge with my bare hands until I could see the wet gray concrete beneath. I squeezed every thought out of my head.

Propping one knee onto the ledge, I crawled up, steadied myself, and stood to a nearly upright position on the narrow space. I looked down at the sparkling world below. Was it the myriad choices that I had made throughout my life, or simply those "slings and arrows of outrageous fortune" that led my footsteps to that ledge? Or was someone else responsible?

Clenching my fists, I stretched my arms up toward the heavens and directed a gut-wrenching cry to the one I could no longer ignore.

"Look at me! Will you look at me? Do you hear me? I despise you for this screwed up life! Do you hear me? Do you hear . . . ?" I turned to the side and dropped down to my hands and knees, lengthwise on the ledge. That's when it finally happened: I began sobbing uncontrollably. It felt both frightening and wonderful. I sank down, my chest to my knees, my face to the surface of the snow. Vapor from my breath circled my face, and I heard myself whisper, "Forgive me . . . please. . . . Whatever I did to deserve this, please forgive me."

I remained motionless for quite some time while listening to the melodic hum of car engines and horns filtering up between the buildings and the chiming of Salvation Army bells, sounding distant enough to be imagined. When I raised my head, I noticed that several feet in front of me on the ledge sat some kind of bundle half-buried in the snow. At first I strained my vision to make it out. Then I tried my best to ignore the thing, but it was as if it were staring at me, wondering what might have provoked my strange behavior. I crawled down off the ledge and walked over to it.

Beneath a hat of snow sat an old, misshapen bag made of a red floral carpet remnant. Although it was damp from the snowfall, the large bag must have been there for quite some time because as I lifted it by its worn leather straps, I saw the concrete beneath it was dry. The bag felt surprisingly light.

I eased myself down on the dry spot, my back to the drop-off, and placed the bag at my side on the ledge. Brushing the snow off the top of it, I uncovered a small brass plaque inscribed with the initials "J. O. E." Above the plaque was a keyhole. A simple brass key dangled from an old gray shoelace knotted to one of the straps.

Unable to pry the bag open, I inserted the key and with a quarter turn, heard a dull click. The top popped open to the width of my hand. Spreading apart the mouth of the bag, I peered inside, but it was too dark to make out if there might be something inside. I shook the bag but didn't hear anything move. Tilting the opening of the bag toward the distant doorway light, I detected a long grayish shape at the bottom. I stuck my hand inside and groped around until my fingers came across the unmistakable texture of a feather.

I removed the slightly tattered, eight-inch-long, white feather. I held it up to the light and ran my fingers along either side of its barbs. It made me think of Jeremy. He had been chosen to play Gabriel in the upcoming Christmas pageant and had been given a pair of giant angel wings to wear for the part. I pictured my daughter, Kelly, prancing around in her cow costume, showing it off to me with such delight on her face. It was only the day before that I had promised them both I'd show up at the pageant on Christmas Eve, which was just four days from now. I held the feather by the quill and twirled it back and forth between my fingers.

It was a moment filled with portent, filled with bitter, fleeting reflections of my entire existence—every moment I'd known. I'd been a disappointment to myself and to everyone I'd ever allowed to come into my life. That conclusion alone should have been enough to send me leaping over the ledge. But the truth was I didn't want to die.

Just as this realization hit me, a warm and hardy gust of wind whipped up from below my feet, ripping the feather out of my hand and over my head. With surprising hand-eye coordination, I instinctively reached up and snatched the rising object, tipping myself off balance. In an instant I was a goner. I flipped backward over the ledge and downward.

I once saw a documentary that substantiated the theory that we humans do, in fact, flash back on the events of our lives moments before we die. But for me there was just one memory, a scene that faded in from the nighttime sky with crystal clarity. One that I didn't remember ever recalling before:

I was six years old, bundled up in my winter coat, maroon corduroy pants, an unfashionable leather hunting cap on my head, and black rubber galoshes on my feet, standing in the snow-covered backyard of my home in Ohio. Untouched by even a hint of a breeze, huge snowflakes slowly danced their way down from the night sky like the aftermath of a pillow fight. I was standing as still as the snowman beside me while my mom, kneeling next to me, finished wrapping my scarf higher around my neck. With my head tilted slightly back and my eyes closed, I stuck my tongue out of my mouth as far as it would go into the cold night air, according to my mom's gentle instruction.

She was explaining to me how God created each individual snowflake to look like no other, just like he created each person to be like no other person. "Every time you catch a snowflake on your tongue, it's like catching a part of Jesus," my mom said. "They'll melt in your mouth and make their way down to your heart, where they'll transform it into a special heart—one that will allow you to truly understand God's love and grace."

My mom's theology always seemed to fall somewhere between Mother Teresa and Mother Goose. This whimsical form of divinity provided me with a rich, if not always accurate, introduction to the meaning of life. My mom died one evening a couple years after that backyard sermon. The morning after she passed away, I awoke to burning ears, badly swollen and tinged with magenta—frostbitten from spending half the night beneath a sky of falling snow, in an attempt to comprehend the love and mercy of my mother's God.

The flashback image ended abruptly, cutting back to the disorienting nighttime blur as I continued my free fall. Strangely enough, maybe because I was drunk, I didn't have a feeling that I was going to die or even hit the ground. But despite the delusion, my body did come crashing down onto the top of an enormous snowdrift in the alley, sliding down to an abrupt halt imbedded in the mountain of powder.

A forty-floor drop and I was still breathing. Granted, they were short breaths until I could reinflate my lungs, but I was alive and holding tight to that feather. And as a bonus, my limbs were all still facing the conventional direction. This was Guinness World Record stuff. Ripley's stuff. Stuff certainly unfamiliar to my life.

Lying on my back, I didn't have a lot of time to contemplate my good fortune because I immediately noticed an object falling at a great velocity toward my head. I attempted to raise my right arm to shield myself, but it was too late: The carpetbag collided with the side of my face.

I felt no pain as I dug myself out of the drift. I didn't even realize that I'd hurt my nose until I saw bloody drippings being absorbed into the hill, creating what looked like a giant, grotesque cherry snow cone. Scooping up a handful of snow, I pressed it against my nose and stared down at the bag lying on its side. It looked lonely and lost but not apologetic. I picked it up and shook off the snow.

I held onto my lapel, forcing my overcoat closed against the wind as I turned the corner out of the alley to the front of the building. The Salvation Army girl had packed it in for the evening, missing out on my miracle.

As I approached the driver's side of my car, I noticed a policeman jotting something down in a small notebook.

"Your car, sir?"

I turned around and realized it wasn't a diary entry he was working on. The huge block of a man had a Dudley Do-Right jaw and eyes set deep within the shadows cast by his Neanderthal brow.

"Yeah. Something wrong, Officer?"

He spoke from beneath a brown walrus mustache in a *Dragnet* voice. "Left your lights on, parked in a no-parking zone."

"Ah."

Taking a long, intimidating stride in my direction, the policeman looked me over, head to toe. Covered with patches of snow, remnants of blood probably still crusting around my nose, and a giant flowered purse tucked under my arm, I looked guilty of any number of things. He began with the obvious.

"You been drinking, sir?"

"I've had a little, yes."

"So I can assume you have no intention of getting behind that wheel?"

"I was just looking to warm up."

He couldn't stop staring at the bag.

"What's with the big purse?"

"What? Oh, this? Nothing. And it's not a purse—it's a bag."

"So what do you keep in the bag, if you don't mind me asking?"

"Nothing. It's empty."

"Care if I take a look?"

Feeling guilty of something—I wasn't sure exactly what—I handed the carpetbag over to the cop. Setting it down on the trunk of my car, he pulled a flashlight from his belt and opened the top of the bag while still keeping a wary eye on me. He flashed the beam of light down into the bag and jiggled it around until he steadied it on one area.

He bit down on the fingertips of his glove, slid his hand out, and cautiously reached into the bag. "Ow—shoot!"

He quickly retracted his hand, shaking it as if he had just been bitten by a small animal with big teeth. I was really nervous now. Dipping his hand back into the bag, the cop brought out a small oval object. It was a cameo brooch. He held it up and flashed his light on the delicate profile of a lovely woman. Her ivory image stood out against a butterscotch-colored background encased in a thin gold frame. The cop looked over to me for an explanation.

"Sorry. I thought it was empty," I said.

"This is very strange," he said, his mustache refusing to move.

"Well, yeah, it is, but I promise you—"

"My wife . . . there was just one thing she asked me to get her this year for Christmas, and I haven't exactly gotten around to shopping yet. And now you turn up with the very thing she asked for. Very strange. It *is* an antique, isn't it?"

"I believe so, yes," I said, mystified and making it up as I went along.

He leaned up against my car, his body relaxing along with his cop attitude. "I realize that this is an unusual request, but . . . any chance you'd be interested in selling me this brooch?"

"No. I mean, you can have it, if you want."

"I can just have it? It isn't hot, is it?" he said, nearly allowing himself to laugh.

"No."

"Well, um, thank you. Tell you what . . . let's get your car moved outta this no-parking zone so you don't get a ticket." He held out his hand for my keys.

I watched him move the car halfway down the block, then hustle back to where I was standing. "Go sober up somewhere warm," he said, dropping the keys back into my palm.

"Okay. Yeah. Thanks, Officer."

He shook my hand and gazed down at the cameo again. "Suzanne's gonna love this." He looked down the street at the carpetbag still sitting on the trunk. "Don't forget your purse." He smiled, turned, and walked off toward his squad car.

Sometimes I would grab lunch at Bertolucci's Restaurant, a couple blocks down from my office. I headed in that direction with my new companion in hand. On the way I paused at a bus stop located beneath a bright street lamp. I sat down on the bench, opened the mouth of the carpetbag as wide as it could tolerate, and poked around inside like a sadistic dentist looking for an abnormality. I found none.

I wanted to believe that somehow I'd simply overlooked the brooch when I first found the feather inside the bag. I was pretty drunk after all. But aside from the bag's unlikely ability to materialize objects, it appeared to possess a talent nearly impossible for me to wrap my logical mind around: the capacity to provide gifts. I snapped the bag closed, walked down to the restaurant, and headed for the bar.

two

SLEIGHT OF HAND

F estive little Christmas lights, dangling everywhere, decked out the cozy Italian restaurant. I sat down in the shadows of the bar area at a table for two, my back to a brick wall. I cupped my hands over a fat candle in a red jar. My frozen ears burned as they began to thaw.

With my hair and clothing still wet from the snow, possibly blood on my face, and the unfashionable carpetbag resting on my lap, I was getting several interesting looks from people. It didn't matter to me. If I weren't hallucinating, I'd just witnessed a couple of supernatural events, and I needed time to find a logical explanation for them.

An instrumental version of "Jingle Bell Rock" was setting the mood for everyone in the bar except me. I wasn't sure if there was a song to fit my scattered frame of mind.

I rubbed my thumb across the worn J. O. E. monogram on the face of the carpetbag. I wanted to open it again, but something stopped me, a feeling, an instinct that said, *Not yet.*

A continuous pinging sound was coming from the table next to me. I looked to my right and saw an attractive woman in her late forties with shoulder length, auburn hair sitting alone, facing the same direction I was, staring out across the room toward the entrance. I wasn't sure if she was drunk or just had really lousy rhythm as she nervously tapped on her exotic drink with one of those colorful little paper parasols. Scattered in front of her on the table were the shredded remains of two other umbrellas. She glanced at her watch, drained her drink, and let out an exasperated sigh.

A middle-aged cocktail waitress, carrying a tray of drinks, appeared between our tables. She looked terribly uncomfortable, bulging out of a skimpy violet outfit at least a size and a half too small. I felt sorry for her. Seemingly in a perpetual state of inhalation, she leaned over next to the umbrella lady. "Can I get you another?"

The woman grabbed her camel hair coat off the chair next to her. "No, I'm fine. But if my invisible date here ever decides to materialize, he'll have a shot of arsenic on me."

The waitress smiled as she set the woman's tab on the table. "Maybe he got held up by the snow," she said.

"Yeah, let's hope it was a small avalanche. Blind date—what the heck was I thinking?" She grabbed the bill, opened her purse, and dug deep.

The waitress turned around toward me.

"And what can I get you, sir?"

"Oh, um, Jack Daniels. No—actually, just a cup of decaf."

"Good enough. I'll be right back," the waitress said, sucking in a considerable amount of air and unavoidably strutting off down the aisle toward the bar.

The angry woman stood up to leave and looked my way as she began buttoning her coat in the middle. "You know, you got it all backwards. You're supposed to arrive sober, leave drunk."

I set the carpetbag on the bench next to me, averting my eyes from her. Apparently she wasn't in the mood to be disregarded twice that evening, because in a saccharine tone she added, "Oh, I'm sorry, I didn't recognize you at first. You're one of *them*, aren't you?"

I moved the bag closer to me and fiddled with the handles, hoping to look preoccupied so that the woman would take the hint. But she wouldn't be denied. "Hey, guy with the goofy bag."

I finally looked over at her.

"I said you're one of them, are you not?"

I could almost see roots splitting down through the soles of her black shoes, pushing their way into the wooden floor and taking hold. The woman was officially planted until she got an answer from me.

"One what?"

"A pholeaziat."

I didn't have a clue what she was suggesting that I might be, but I was pretty sure it wasn't a term of endearment.

"A phony sleazy rat," she explained. "You're one of 'em, all right. Know how I know? I'll tell you—because you're a man. Admit it. You're a pholeaziat, right?"

This stranger and I had both consumed more than our share of alcohol and rejection that evening, so I understood her anger. I stared into the candle flame, and the image of Kathy's expression as she sat in the rocking chair reappeared to me. "Yeah. Yeah, that I am."

My admission of guilt seemed to catch her totally off guard. "You are?" She was quiet for a second, then said, "No, see, when someone says something rude to you, you're supposed to be rude back. It's only common courtesy."

She stood there in the middle of the aisle for a good ten seconds just looking lost. I searched the room for the waitress, hoping my coffee would arrive soon. Then, as the music floating in the air segued into "The Christmas Song"—sung by Nat King Cole—the woman looked up and took a deep breath, like she was inhaling the silky opening melody line.

Chestnuts roasting on an open fire . . .

She exhaled, and calm seemed to take hold of her.

"Look, I'm sorry," she said. "I'm not usually nearly this obnoxious, really. It's just . . . I'm really sorry."

"You don't need to apologize," I said.

"But I do. My name's Maggie Olson." She held out her hand, and I shook it.

"I'm David."

"Do you mind?" Maggie gestured toward the empty chair across from me. I wasn't really in the mood for company, but as I shrugged my shoulders, she plopped herself down. She had an attractive face, but one that looked like it had been ticked off for years. A heavy coat of mascara framed large green eyes that didn't need the enhancement.

The waitress arrived and set the cup of coffee in front of me. "There you go."

"Thank you."

She turned to Maggie, who politely waved her off. It seemed I had little choice, so I took a sip of my coffee, set it down, and gave Maggie my full attention.

She began with a sigh. "I hate this time of year. It tries to turn you into some kind of a softy. The lights, the smells . . . everybody pretending to be in such an exceedingly pleasant mood . . . and then there're these songs. Nat King Cole just messes with your heart. Who needs it, right?"

She was talking to me as if I were an old friend. I couldn't help but squirm in my chair. "Not me," she continued. "Come tomorrow, I'll be lying out on a sunny beach in Miami, without a snowflake or a Christmas tree or a Santa Claus in sight. Just need to pick up a pair of sunglasses, and I'll be all set." She eyed the carpetbag at my side. "Looks like you might have the same idea. So where're you headed?"

Seizing the opportunity to further test the properties of the bag, and my own mental health, I slid the candle and my coffee off to the side and set the carpetbag on top of the table. I unlatched the lock and eased the carpetbag over in front of her. "You tell me."

"Is this some kind of a game?"

"Go ahead. Look inside."

She glanced down into the narrow opening then pried open the bag and briefly dipped her head deeper into its mouth like a reluctant lion tamer. "Ah, a light packer. It's empty. I don't get it."

I leaned back, confused and even strangely disappointed. Maggie closed the bag and pushed it back over to me.

"Forget it," I said. "I thought that maybe . . ." I began to sense something. I stared at the carpetbag. Maybe it was my imagination or wishful thinking, but I felt a presence inside the bag.

"You thought that maybe what?"

I touched the side of the bag with my fingertips, gently stroking the nap. The presence began to take on form, a shape, narrow and angular. I didn't know how I knew, but as sure as Maggie was sitting across from me, there was an object inside that bag.

Without looking in, I dropped my hand down into the bag

like one of those mechanical claw machines. My fingers found an object along the bottom: smooth, hard, pointy. They closed down around it. My hand trembled as I lifted out a pair of sunglasses with pink cat's eye frames.

Maggie broke into a smile and applause. I just stared at the sunglasses, feeling like they could vanish from my hand at any second.

"Whoa! Fabulous! So you're a magician! Not bad. It's no bunny rabbit, but still, I'm very impressed."

There was no more room for doubt. The magic was real, and it scared the snot out of me. I gingerly handed the sunglasses to Maggie. "I think these are meant for you."

"Really? Not exactly my style, but thanks. So how'd you do it? Or is it some kind of trade secret?"

I eased the top of the carpetbag closed, ready for the show to be over.

"You all right?" Maggie asked. "You look a little pukey. Maybe if you showed me another trick—"

"I'm not a magician."

"Oh, don't sell yourself short like that. You have real talent. Not just anybody can—"

All my confusion turned to anger as I leaned forward and grabbed Maggie by the wrist. "Listen to me. I am not taking a trip. I am not a magician. And I am not crazy!"

"Crazy? You?" Maggie shook loose of my grasp and quickly scooted her chair away from the table. "No, no, of course you're not crazy," she said, standing up. "Who could possibly accuse you of being crazy? Gotta go." She turned to leave.

"Wait!" I said, rising to my feet. "I'm sorry. Please, don't go."

Maggie stopped, her eyes fixed on the exit. "Why not? I mean, why would I want to endure even more abuse than I've already experienced this evening?" She looked over at me. "Why should I stay?"

"Because I don't want to be alone in this."

She closed her eyes and shook her head.

I leaned on the table in an attempt to calm the tremors in my body.

"How do I know you're not some kind of lunatic or something?" she asked.

"You don't. But I'm not."

"Yeah, well, I'm gonna need some proof."

I removed my wallet from my back pocket, flipped it opened to a plastic sleeve insert holding a small family portrait taken last year, and stuck it in front of her face.

"This is your proof?"

"This is my wife, Kathy. And these are my kids, Jeremy and Kelly."

"So you can procreate. Big deal. Lunatics are reproducing all over the world as we speak."

I closed the wallet, tucked it back into my pocket, and sat down. "You're right. You should go."

After a moment Maggie sat down sidesaddle on the chair, assuring herself a fast getaway if I should suddenly go berserk again. I was happy she'd decided to stay and let her know with a smile. "So why aren't you sharing your little psychotic episode with that pretty wife of yours?"

It was more information than I wanted to provide. But after a few futile attempts to get the words out, I finally said, "We're kind of separated."

"There's a shocker . . . sorry." Maggie dragged the candle over in front of her. "You said you didn't want to be alone in this. Alone in what?"

There was something in her eyes as she said *sorry* . . . they softened somehow. I decided to tell her my story. Most of it. "Less than an hour ago I was on the rooftop of an office building a few blocks away from here."

"And what were you doing there?"

"It's where I work. I was just taking a break—getting some air."

I felt horrible that I had to begin with a lie, but I didn't see that I had much choice.

"You have lousy work hours."

"Yeah, well, anyway . . . I noticed this bag sitting on the ledge, and I picked it up."

"So whose is it?"

"I don't know. But that's not the point."

"What is the point?"

"I know this is going to sound crazy . . . really crazy . . . but one moment the bag is empty, and the next . . . it's not."

She looked at me, not like I was nuts, but possibly just mistaken. "Maybe there's a hidden lining or something."

"No. Trust me. I checked a dozen times."

"Well, there has to be a logical explanation for it."

"Unfortunately that's only half the weirdness of it. Not only do things materialize, these things seem to be . . . gifts."

"Gifts?" She reached over and traced the outline of a flower on the carpetbag.

"Yeah. Things people need. You said you needed sunglasses for your trip; *bam*—they showed up."

"Yeah, but—"

"And earlier there was a cop who pulled some jewelry out of here—exactly what his wife wanted for Christmas."

"Hey, take it outside," boomed a voice just down the aisle and behind the bar. Maggie's focus shifted to the bartender. I looked past her shoulder. The bartender was leaning across the bar, reprimanding a guy in a brown flannel shirt who was in a heated discussion with a well-dressed man who had a girl hanging on his arm.

I touched Maggie's hand, and she quickly turned back toward me.

"Look, it's not that I don't want to believe you," she said. "It's just that I live in the real world, and in the real world, things don't just materialize out of thin air." Maggie lifted the bag up off the table. "And this bag is definitely empty."

To prove her point, Maggie turned the bag upside down. A semi-frozen slab of raw meat fell from the bag onto the table with a thud.

Maggie dropped the bag like it was on fire. "Holy cripes." She cautiously reached over and poked the steak a few times like she was checking to see if it was real. She picked up the cold hunk of meat with two fingers, and held it up.

At that moment we heard a *whack!* and the guy in the flannel shirt flew back toward us, landing at Maggie's feet.

Conversations around the tables fell silent as everyone turned their attention to the scuffle. The guy on the floor covered his eye. The suited man who had knocked him down approached and stood over him like Ali over Liston. "And if you ever talk to my girl like that again, I swear, I'll kill you!"

The bartender hustled over and grabbed the man by the arm, "Let's go, buddy."

"Nobody talks to my girl like that," he said.

The bartender pulled the man away from our table and escorted him and his angry girlfriend out the door. Our cocktail waitress dashed over to our table and bent down to check the guy out. "You all right?"

"Yeah, I'm fine," the guy said, still covering his eye. "All I said was that I thought she was pretty."

The waitress moved the guy's hand away from his face to get a better look at the damage. His eye was already beginning to swell shut and discolor. "We need to get something cold on that eye right away."

Maggie still held the frosty steak pinched delicately between her fingers. She looked down at the waitress. "Will this do?"

The waitress gazed up and stared blankly at her for a moment; then she grabbed the steak from Maggie and placed it against the man's eye.

Maggie flashed a nauseated look my way. "Get me out of here."

I dropped a few bucks on the table, took Maggie's arm, and we were off. A rush of adrenaline shot through my body, assuring me that I wasn't crazy after all. My brain was functioning just fine. It was only the world that was spinning a bit off-kilter.

three

THE REASON
FOR THE SEASON

Slipping out of the restaurant with Maggie, I half expected the world to be suddenly transformed into shades of black and white, and for us to run into Rod Serling standing in the shadows, thin gray smoke rising from the cigarette in his hand as he uttered the words: "A dimension not only of sight and sound, but of mind . . ."

With the carpetbag tucked under my arm, I looked down the street in the general direction of my car.

"So what happens now?" Maggie asked, pulling a pair of brown leather gloves from her pockets.

"I don't know."

Maybe it was the fall. Maybe it did kill me after all, like it certainly should have. Could it be that this was my afterlife or some kind of postmortem test? Maybe all my actions were being monitored, judged by a higher power. Maybe even Maggie wasn't real. And maybe the contents of the bag and how I reacted to them were somehow going to be instrumental in determining my salvation or something. My thinking was starting to sound as convoluted as my mother's. I didn't dare share these thoughts with Maggie. Of course, if I were right about her not being real, what would it matter what she thought? Maybe I just needed a good slap upside my head.

"You know that I can't simply say good-bye to you after what just happened, don't you?" Maggie said, cramming her glove over her hand. I nodded. "My car's right around here somewhere. Maybe we could go to my apartment . . . try to sort this thing out."

I was pretty sure I had sobered up enough to drive home, but judging from Maggie's futile attempt at matching up fingers with holes, she had a ways to go. She tried to focus her eyes on her glove, stuck on her hand like some kind of a rooster puppet. "That's not right, is it?"

Even though I found Maggie to be abrasive in many ways, the truth was I didn't want to be alone with that carpetbag. It both fascinated and frightened me, and I didn't want exclusive responsibility for its future or mine.

So after chipping a layer of ice off the windshield of Maggie's Saturn, we headed toward her apartment. The bag rested calmly on her lap as she sat in the passenger's seat calling out directions. When the heater began to warm us up, Maggie and I attempted to make sense of it all. But there were no explanations, cosmic or otherwise, to explain the peculiar behavior of the seemingly normal piece of antique luggage.

"I have to tell you . . ." Maggie said, "when I left my apartment earlier, this was not one of the scenarios that I had imagined for the evening."

"I heard you mention something about a blind date to the waitress."

"Yeah. He probably caught a glimpse of me through the window and ran off into the night screaming."

From my peripheral vision I could detect Maggie glancing over at me, possibly hoping I'd challenge her assessment of why she'd been stood up, and I nearly waited too long for my reaction to sound sincere. "I can't imagine that was the case."

In a deep, cartoon voice Maggie said, "Bigzaney4."

"What?"

"That's his screen name. Should have been a clue, huh? Lonely, desperate losers — that's how I always viewed those people who would hook up with online dating services. And then somehow, one night, my curiosity got the best of me, and I mutated into one. His real name was Frank. Seemed nice enough. He didn't post a picture of himself, but said he looked a little like Gary Cooper. 'Fond of Italian food, Motown music, and small animals. A fan of Nick Hornby and Daffy Duck.' Said he was a movie nut. And when he mentioned that *Casablanca* was his favorite, I thought maybe, just maybe . . . whatever. It was a stupid idea from the start."

Twinges of guilt hit me like pub darts. I was about to visit the apartment of an available woman. And even though I had no real attraction to Maggie — and no intentions of passion — it felt like I was cheating on Kathy. I had to remind myself that, at the moment, Kathy couldn't have cared less. I tried not to let that thought bring me down all over again. But she remained in my head.

Given the whirlwind of events twisting my life around, I found it hard to believe that only the night before I had driven over to Kathy's church to watch Jeremy and Kelly rehearse in the Christmas pageant. The church marquee out by the curb offered its December advertising hook: The Reason for the Season. I had pulled up next to it and slid the gearshift into park.

Kathy's involvement in the church had begun innocently enough when one of her fellow teachers at Roosevelt Elementary School suggested Kathy join her for Sunday morning service. A couple months later, during one of the many lulls in our dinner conversation, Kathy told me that she had become a born-again Christian. I think she expected me to be upset, but I was happy for her. She had found something to fill the growing void she had spoken of so often. Unfortunately, shortly after this announcement, she had me agreeing to give up the comfort of my Sunday-morning-football recliner for a seat next to her in a less-than-comfortable pew.

To my surprise Pastor Neal Larson wasn't at all like those TV evangelists that I'd run across while channel surfing. He didn't have strange hair or a weird accent or a bizarre speaking style. His sermons utilized his sharp wit and casual yet articulate delivery in a manner that was quite engaging and thought provoking. And the majority of the choir's worship songs were contemporary and entertaining when compared to the "Old Rugged Cross" style of old-fashioned gospel hymns that I remembered struggling to stay awake through as a kid.

But when the sermon and the music stopped and heads bowed to pray, my mind would immediately take a walk. At first I tried to fool myself into believing that it was simply my inability to focus. But I knew better. My mind wandered in order to avoid a confrontation with the one who'd left me standing out in the cold all those years ago. Much to Kathy's dismay, I vacated that pew for good after three weeks, renewing my long-standing arrangement with God that I would stay out of his house and he would stay out of mine.

So instead of meeting up with Kathy inside the church to watch our kids rehearse that night, I remained outside, trying to hold up my end of the bargain seated in my car with the heater blasting and a bottle-shaped brown paper bag in my lap. But it wasn't that easy. Seeing as I was driving, I wasn't going to be able to get high enough to drink away the feelings of guilt. The plan was to wait in the car until I saw people filing out of the church, then approach Kathy and give her some off-the-cuff excuse for my being late. Improvised excuses always sounded more convincing than ones I'd rehearsed.

I wanted it to at least look like I was making an effort to see the rehearsal, and the truth was I did want to see my kids. Though I have to admit, for some reason I didn't take as much pride in their accomplishments as most parents did with their children. Not that I was much good at being a grown-up or being emotionally mature. But I was exceptionally lousy at being a kid and getting down on their level. For me there was this big moat between adulthood and childhood for which I lacked either a rowboat or a drawbridge. The fact is I didn't remember much about my own kidhood, and on an emotional level, somewhere along the way, my inner child must have just up and left, run away, unhappy in the home that was me.

I began to rationalize that it wasn't exactly a church service or anything, and I did want to be there for my kids. I checked my watch—eight thirty. I'd only be a half hour late if I went in.

I silenced the engine and stepped out into the street. Glancing up at the steeple atop the church, I noticed the snow had stopped falling. The drop in temperature had turned the mass of slushy footprints on the sidewalk to ice. I slowly walked up to the front door.

In the foyer I stomped the snow off my sneakers and peeked through the small, yellow tinted windows in the doors leading to the sanctuary.

The dark room was lit at the far end where a nativity scene was set up on stage. Little kids in costumes of kings, shepherds, and various animals gathered in a semicircle on the straw covered stage. I squinted but couldn't pick out Jeremy or Kelly in the bunch.

In the middle of the group, a tall woman in blue jeans and a bright pink blouse stood alongside the manger.

I slipped unnoticed through the double doors and into the rear of the dark sanctuary. The curtains had been drawn over all the stained glass windows that lined either side of the room, making the church look less holy, less intimidating.

About a dozen adults sat scattered around in the pews up front, but it was too dark to locate Kathy. I was about to make my way down to the front when the woman on stage said to the kids, "Great job today. Give yourselves a hand." She led them in applauding themselves. It was over. *The rehearsal was over*. I could have sworn Kathy told me it started at eight o'clock.

"I'll see you all back here for another rehearsal in two days," the lady in pink said. The children sprang to their feet and jumped off the stage to rejoin their parents.

I was about to sneak into the back pew when I heard a man's voice calling from a few aisles in front of me.

"David." Pastor Neal, a portly man dressed in a powder blue cardigan sweater and tan Dockers, rose from his seat with a smile and walked up to me. His perpetual grin always gave the impression that he was about to break into laughter. "It's good to see you," he said.

"Nice seeing you again, Pastor."

"I'm afraid you've missed the rehearsal," Neal said, "but Jeremy and Kelly did great."

I spotted Kathy talking with another mom in front of the stage under a harsh blue light. Even after eleven years together, standing there across the room under less-than-flattering lighting conditions, Kathy looked like someone I'd want to meet for the first time all over again.

Neal noticed that I had spotted Kathy. "She's a terrific person, David. We've really appreciated the energy and commitment Kathy's brought to this church." There was an awkward pause. "Listen, David . . . if you ever reconsider and want the three of us to get together to talk, I'm here for you."

The overhead lights in the sanctuary came on. I looked down toward the front and located Jeremy. He had told me that he was going to be some sort of angel in this play, and sure enough, there he stood, wearing a white robe and a pair of large white wings on his back. Kelly, dressed in a brown and white spotted cow costume, was draped around her mom's legs, a sure sign that she was ready to leave.

"I don't claim to have all the answers as to how to put a marriage back together," the pastor continued, "but I do know that it starts by focusing on a power greater than any of us. The Scriptures assure us that with him, all things are possible."

"I appreciate your concern, Pastor, but to tell you the truth, I'm doing just fine these days believing in only what these eyes of mine can see."

"Are you, David?"

I wasn't certain if it was a rhetorical question or not. I didn't really care. I was just happy the conversation was ending as I focused on Kathy and the kids walking up the aisle toward me. Kathy looked at me blankly, with her head tipped to the side, forcing her blonde hair to curl onto her shoulder. Jeremy ran a couple steps ahead of her and up to me.

"Did you see me fly, Dad?"

"Hey, how you doing, kiddo?"

"*Did* you see him fly, David?" Kathy asked. Lately she began every conversation with me like we were already in the middle of an argument.

I looked over at Pastor Neal. He returned a look that defied me to lie.

"Didn't you tell me that it started at eight?"

"Seven. I said seven o'clock. So you didn't see Jeremy fly or Kelly do her cow?"

"No. I'm afraid I missed it—sorry." Jeremy's disappointment was less obvious than Kathy's.

"I saw you fly, Jeremy," Neal said, patting my son's head. "And you were magnificent. The angels themselves would delight in your performance."

Kathy leaned over to me and whispered, "Your priorities never fail to amaze me, David."

I felt a tug on my pant leg and looked down at Kelly in her costume. "I'm a cow, Daddy."

I just stared down at her without a response in my head, but Neal squatted down next to her and gently poked her black painted cow nose. "And you look *moovelous*, my dear." Kelly let out a giggle.

"They really wanted you to be here," Kathy said.

"We've set up quite an elaborate harness rigging to enable the angel Gabriel here to fly down to deliver his message to the virgin

Mary," Neal said. "In fact, here's the guy who makes it possible."

A big, burly guy carrying a couple folding chairs walked up the aisle toward us. Neal grabbed him by the arm.

"This is Terry Jackson," the pastor said. I nodded and shook the man's hand. "And this is David, Jeremy's dad."

"Nice to meet you." Terry's voice was about an octave higher than his appearance might have predicted. "Jeremy here does all the work. I just grab the cable and hang on."

"He's being very modest," Neal said. "It's very tricky and takes considerable practice to make the effect look convincing."

Terry smiled. "Well, it was nice meeting you, David. You've got a couple great kids there." He continued on his way.

I spotted a white feather on the floor, picked it up, and handed it to Jeremy. "You don't want to be losing too many of these, sport, or you'll never get off the ground. So I can't believe you actually fly in this play."

Without missing a beat, Pastor Neal placed his hand on my shoulder and smiled. "I guess you'll just have to wait for visual confirmation." He could really be a smart aleck for a preacher. Maybe that's what I liked about him most.

"You *will* be making an appearance for the actual pageant, won't you, David?" Kathy asked.

"I promise you I will be right here on Christmas Day to watch you guys."

Slowly pulling Kelly in closer to her side, Kathy said, "The pageant's on Christmas Eve." I felt like a fool.

"Can you come over and help us trim the tree tonight, Dad?" Jeremy asked.

"Sure," I said.

Kathy put her arm around Jeremy. "It's getting a little late,

Jeremy. Maybe your Dad can come by tomorrow night. Unless, of course, he has to work late."

"I'll be there."

I had said it with conviction because I'd meant it. In fact, I'd spent all day at the office looking forward to it. Sitting in front of my computer screen redesigning a cartoon dog, I stopped to indulge myself, to imagine the evening with my family. Though Kathy never cared much for the taste of eggnog, she knew I loved it. I'd hoped that the spirit of the season might prod her heart, and she'd greet me at the door with a smile and a tall, cold glass of the stuff. Maybe she'd even give me a kiss hello. And the kids, they'd be excited to see me and would take my hands and lead me over to the tree where, as a family, we'd string the lights and hang the ornaments, drape tinsel one strand at a time, just the way Kathy liked. We'd listen to Christmas songs, and we'd laugh like crazy. It would be great. I was going to make sure our time together as a family was rich and meaningful. This time I was going to make things right.

But I had lost track of time at the office Christmas party, and I hadn't counted on the snowstorm or the traffic, so when I finally pulled up to the house and stepped out of my car and saw the fully decorated tree there in the bay window, I just wanted to spread my arms, catch a snowy breeze, and fly away for good.

four

STAGE FRIGHT

After a short drive we pulled up in front of Maggie's place and entered her apartment complex through a glass door displaying a plastic green wreath covered with small, blinking white lights.

We climbed the stairs to the second floor and walked down the hallway, the brown sculptured carpeting giving off a new acrylic smell that for some reason made me feel unwelcome. Maggie unlocked her apartment door, and I and the carpetbag followed her inside.

She flipped on the entryway light, revealing a small, comfortable, open-air apartment furnished in early IKEA. The place was a veritable showcase of wicker and blond furniture and was immaculately clean—like Maggie was expecting company. And maybe she had been. But Bigzaney4 I was not.

A calico cat greeting Maggie with a soft meow and an arching back turned in a circle beside the hem of her coat. "Say hello to Garbo." She bent down and stroked the cat's back. "Her partner in crime is around here somewhere. You like cats?"

"Not particularly."

"Really? Why not?" Maggie walked over to a small living-room area and turned on a lamp with a yellow paper shade shaped in a geodesic dome.

"I just don't."

"Well, you're missing out on one of the great pets of all time. Can I get you some coffee?"

"Only if you're going to have some yourself."

On her way to the open kitchen, she stripped off her coat and draped it across the back of the couch.

"Yeah, I guess I have a real love for animals in general. Instant okay?"

"Fine."

I set the carpetbag down on a coffee table, nudging a group of magazines meticulously fanned out, displaying *Newsweek* on top. I opened up the bag, checking to see if it had been busy working miracles while we weren't paying attention. It hadn't.

The microwave hummed in the kitchen as I wandered around the room. I spotted a second cat prowling behind the leaves of a grape ivy, which sat on one of two built-in bookshelves filled to capacity. The shelf at eye level exclusively held paperbacks while the shelves directly above and below held hard covers.

Maggie called out from the kitchen. "You should know that I live alone. So if you run into anybody else around here, just hit 'em with a lamp or the nearest heavy, blunt object."

I've always been suspicious of people who live alone, who pick out their furniture, food, and entertainment without needing to compromise. They are a different breed. One I didn't understand. And though I'd been living that lifestyle for several months, it wasn't me. Never would be.

Several Maxfield Parrish illustrations hung on the limited wall space. I walked up to a summertime countryside scene behind glass, displayed in a thin, antique frame of golden oak, its delicate beadwork still intact. A quaint, white wooden house in the distance nestled among giant, spreading oaks with powerful cumulous clouds rising behind them in a cobalt blue sky. All three elements reflected with sharp clarity in the small grassy-banked lake that curved into the foreground. Parrish knew his audience — dreamers. His scenes were so idealized in their natural settings and yet so realistically executed in brilliant, vibrant colors that the viewer, particularly if he were the sort given to daydreams, couldn't possibly help but take that emotional step inside Parrish's world. I took the opportunity to escape myself.

"Sheltering Oaks," Maggie called out from around the corner of the kitchen, noticing me staring into the scene. "One of my favorites," she added.

Nothing Maggie had revealed in her personality up to this point had given me any indication that she'd be a member of Parrish's fan club. She was nuts and bolts; Parrish was smoke and light.

"You like Parrish?" she asked, leaning on the kitchen counter, waiting for the water to boil.

"Yeah, I guess."

"I love his landscapes. But I can do without the ones that have people in them."

Those were my favorites. I didn't understand the point of a painting without somebody in it. I especially never cared for a still life. Fruit — who cares to look at fruit?

Maggie pulled the mugs from the microwave and stirred in the coffee. "At least take off your coat; act like you're going to stay awhile."

I strolled over to the coffee table, removed my coat, folded it over onto itself, and dropped it onto a rocker. Then I sat down on the edge of an angular blond chair evidently designed more for aesthetic appeal than functional comfort. Maybe the chair and I had something in common. "You like living alone?" I asked Maggie as she approached with two mugs of coffee.

"What's not to like? No one to clean up after, argue with, deal with. No one to have to cook for or shove back over to his side of the bed." She set a mug down in front of me and perched herself across from me on the edge of the couch.

"Thanks."

"So what about you?" she asked. "You mentioned you were separated. How long now?"

"Three months."

"Living alone isn't so bad, is it?"

I hated it. "It's all right, I suppose."

"It takes time, but it grows on you. I mean, what's the worst thing about it? It gets a little lonely every once in a while. Big deal."

I didn't feel like telling Maggie, but the worst part about living alone for me was when something good happened. Like when I'd be watching TV, a comedy usually, and one of the characters would say something so funny that I'd laugh out loud. That moment right after I laughed—I wasn't crazy about that moment.

Maggie leaned forward on her elbows and rested her face in her hands to peer into the bag, her perfume drifting across the table toward me. It was a scent that Kathy would have found too sweet and heavy to have ever considered wearing—a fragrance that could have easily been misinterpreted as trying too hard.

"Maybe it's run out of stuff," Maggie suggested, sitting upright.

"It's not that I haven't had roommates," she said then, picking up on the subject again. "In fact I was married once . . . a while ago. Lasted a couple years. Ended before we could do any real damage by having kids."

She paused and seemed to be waiting for me to ask her what happened. She couldn't wait that long.

"I used to think we broke up because he brought so much baggage with him into the relationship. And I'm not talking about the carry-on variety. He checked in about four bags over the limit. But eventually I understood he wasn't entirely the problem."

"So what was the problem?"

"I realized that I was still in love with another guy. Someone I knew long before I met my husband." Maggie looked up at the ceiling like she had just spotted a harmless spider crossing the white stucco terrain. I had a feeling she didn't really want to talk about it but couldn't help herself.

"His name was Roger. I met him my freshman year at a Christmas frat party down at Southern University. He was a senior. We hit it off right away. He was handsome, funny, polite . . ."

"Groovy?" I asked, guessing she might be talking about the sixties.

"Actually he was kind of nerdy—black Buddy Holly glasses and all. But I found him oddly endearing. Near the end of the party, we found ourselves in a doorway under a bunch of mistletoe. Well, actually, I managed to maneuver him over there without him suspecting anything. And when he noticed the mistletoe, he swept his brown wavy hair off his forehead and asked me, 'Margaret, would it be all right if I kissed you?' That killed me. It was so charming! I had wanted to kiss him from the moment I first saw him walk through the door. And so I leaned forward and kissed him . . . and he held onto me and whispered into my ear, 'Meet you here a year from now.'"

Maggie stared into the space between us like it was a dimension that she'd visited before.

"We were together every day through the spring until he graduated. He was drafted in the summer. Sent to Vietnam in the fall. He was due home on leave for Christmas. But I guess God had other plans for him." She lifted the coffee to her lips, but she didn't drink. "Guess you can figure out the rest, huh." Maggie's eyes began to tear up as she set the cup down on the table. But then she forced a smile and directed her attention to the bag again. "If you want the truth, this thing really gives me the willies," she said, falling back into the cushions of the couch.

Was it dead or simply playing possum? One thing for certain, our staring at it wasn't helping to bring it back to life. I wasn't even sure I wanted this curiosity to wake. But I did wish I were sharing this theater of the absurd with Kathy. If the experience had managed to bond two strangers, surely in some way it would have brought Kathy and me closer together.

"I wonder what something like this would fetch on eBay?" Maggie said. "Magic bag — can conjure up jewelry, exotic eyewear, and beef products."

I zoomed in on the name plaque once again. "So who do you think this J. O. E. person might be?"

"I don't think I want to know. But hopefully he's not related to Satan."

"What are you talking about?"

Maggie lay down on the couch, stretching out on her back, revealing her long, shapely legs. "Well, I know that everything the bag's had to offer so far has been pretty innocent and all, but who's to say the next thing that pops out isn't a severed head or something?"

I leaned forward and cautiously closed the top of the bag with my fingertips. Maggie seemed to get a kick out of my response. She grinned and rolled over onto her side, sliding one arm down along the contour of her risen hip while tucking her other arm under a couple of throw pillows supporting her head. It seemed an inappropriately provocative pose for a business meeting such as ours. Then again, maybe I was reading too much into her body language. "So what was it with your wife?" she asked.

"What?" Maggie could change subjects at the speed of light.

"What did you do to send her and the kids packing?"

"In the first place, if you have to know—"

"And I do."

"She wasn't the one to leave."

"Ah, she kicked you out. How come?"

It was none of Maggie's business. I knew she was just trying to be playful, but I wasn't in the mood.

"What was it—drinking problem? Drugs? Anger management issues? Pornography addiction? Or did you find your secretary a little too desirable to pass up? If you don't mind me asking."

I did. "Why do you assume it was my fault?"

"Was it?"

I just sat there, unresponsive, feeling my butt going numb on that stupid chair.

Wrinkling up her nose, Maggie said, "If you don't want to share, that's fine. I'm just killing time until something else shows up in this bag of yours. And by the way, if you have any influence over this thing, you might drop the hint that a winning lotto ticket would come in very handy. One more guess . . . you fell out of love."

I almost didn't say it. "Apparently that's not possible."

"What do you mean? Why not?"

I had a feeling this interrogation wasn't going to pass any time soon, so I took a step out of my comfort zone to be perfectly honest. "Because you have to know what love is before you can fall out of it. And according to my wife . . ."

Maggie sat up on the couch like a terrier awakened by the doorbell. It probably shouldn't have surprised me, but there it was again — that look. Her high arching, perfectly plucked brown eyebrows scooted ever so slightly toward the middle of her forehead. I'd taken one step too far — where solid ground left off and quicksand began. I immediately regretted having given in to her.

"She actually accused you of that?"

"She wasn't trying to be mean."

"Yeah, well, who the heck really knows what love's all about, right?" I knew she said it for my sake, and I appreciated it. "Could be this wife of yours — what's her name?"

"Kathy."

"Right. Could be Kathy just wasn't, you know, the right one for you."

She *was* the right one. I'd always known that.

"You'll meet someone else."

I had no interest in disappointing someone new.

Maggie didn't say anything for a few moments. "You think she's right, don't you? I mean about you not knowing what love is."

"Maybe."

"Why?"

"You have a degree in psychology, do you?"

"Freud, Dear Abby, *Peanuts* — read 'em all. I think that qualifies me."

Maybe it was easier because I'd just met Maggie. Or maybe it had something to do with our connection to the bag, or maybe it was because it was so late and the coffee was kicking in. I proceeded to do the unnatural. "Ever feel like life is this play going on in front of you?" I stared at the carpetbag, not willing to risk the chance of seeing those eyebrows of hers shift any farther north.

"You mean . . . do I ever feel removed . . . detached?"

"Yeah."

"Sure. Sometimes. I think everybody does from time to time."

"Almost as far back as I can remember, that's how it's felt. I'm pretty sure I must have fallen to earth one day when I was a kid, sent here only to observe, not to participate. Like life is a performance. And I'm just somewhere in the audience, sitting in the dark, watching, taking it all in."

"So what keeps you from leaping onto the stage and taking a part?"

I wasn't sure. I'd always avoided analyzing it. "I think I'm afraid I wouldn't know how to act once I got up there. Or that I'd realize that it's not my play to be in, that I just didn't belong on the stage."

"And so you're comfortable in the loge, are you?"

"When it comes to dealing with most people, yeah, I suppose I am. But when it comes to my family . . . I'm crazy about my wife. And my kids, they're the best. But as much as I've wanted to really get close to them, to be there for them, to love them, I can't. They're just out of reach. And I feel paralyzed in this seat, unable to do a blasted thing about it. So no . . . this place in the dark will never feel comfortable." I felt like I was bleeding from my mouth. I'd said way too much. Yet there was more I could have said. The truth was it wasn't just that I felt uncomfortable in my own skin—it was deeper than that. Alzheimer's victims suffer because of electrical misfiring of the connections in the brain—a break in communication between the present consciousness and the area of the brain that stores memories. That's how it was with me, except my misfiring took place between my head and my heart, maybe even between my heart and my soul. But while medical science inched closer to solving the mystery of dementia, I remained clueless.

Maggie looked like she was about to tell me how lousy she felt for me. I wanted something to leap out of the bag at that second. Something so remarkable or outrageous or ridiculous that its appearance could totally negate the emotional nakedness I'd just revealed. It's what I needed. But instead, the bag sat lifeless, either unaware of my inner thoughts or simply uncooperative. So I remained sitting across from Maggie, her silence blaring in my ears.

five

THE GIFT THAT KEEPS ON GIVING

A blinding white panorama washed away any sign of a horizon line as I found myself skiing downhill at a rapid clip. I was pretty sure I was dreaming because I had no idea how to ski during the waking hours. With the wind whistling past me and my body shedding its weight, the run felt effortless and exhilarating, like flying—a rush too euphoric to terminate with the opening of my eyes. But the experience quickly turned treacherous, as I realized I was unable to slow down. Up ahead, an indistinguishable gray figure appeared directly in my path. In an instant I was upon it, digging my skis into the snow and spraying a wave of powder as I swerved to the side, narrowly avoiding a collision. I skidded to a halt, turned around, and there, standing right in front of me, was Kathy. She was wearing a fire-engine red cardigan sweater, her features softened by the glow of the snow. "Kathy, what are you doing here?"

She didn't speak but smiled lovingly and leaned in close to me as if to whisper something in my ear. I felt a strange sensation on my cheek.

I woke up to Garbo's sandpaper tongue lapping up a line of drool that spilled over the corner of my lip. I was too startled to be embarrassed as I stiff-armed the cat away.

"Sorry about that," Maggie said in a foggy morning voice from the kitchen. "Garbo has this thing about drool." Okay, *now* I was embarrassed. "Not to imply that you drool. Or that I do, for that matter." Now everyone was embarrassed except the cat.

I didn't even remember falling asleep, but there I was on the couch, the orange pillow now under my head, a patchwork quilt half-covering my body, still dressed in yesterday's clothes. The morning light sliced through blond wooden blinds, filling the room and striping the walls. I propped myself up on one elbow and muscled my eyelids open far enough to locate Maggie behind the kitchen counter. Her hair wet and wavy, she was wrapped up in a white robe and poured dry cat food nuggets from a small bag into a lime green ceramic bowl.

"Can I get you some breakfast?" she asked.

"Not if that's it." I yawned.

Maggie smiled my way. Garbo bounded across the room and sprang onto the counter, nudging the bowl. "I usually eat a small breakfast," Maggie said. "Generally just some toast and fruit. You're welcome to the same. But if you'd prefer, I did manage to scrounge up a box of Cap'n Crunch left over from when I babysat my nephews a few months ago." She held up the bright yellow box and shook it. It didn't make a sound. Here was a difficult choice. "It has Crunchberries," she added in a singsong voice, as if that might be a determining factor.

"As long as it still floats, I'll eat it." Sitting up, I noticed the carpetbag was no longer resting on the coffee table. I scanned the room for it.

"It's over by the door," Maggie said, reading my mind.

"Then it wasn't all just a bizarre dream?"

Maggie turned the Captain's box upside down over a bowl and pinched the sides in an attempt to coax the cereal out. "As far as I'm concerned, none of it ever happened."

"You can just do that, huh?"

"I have no choice — I can't afford the therapy sessions." Red and yellow clumps of cereal resembling the trashed remains of a school kid's model of an atom fell out of the box.

"So you haven't looked inside it this morning?"

"Looked inside what?" Maggie flashed a smile, but I could tell she was serious about erasing the memory of last night. I completely understood her position.

Only time and a fading memory could ever allow me to write off the incident as imagination run amuck. Or maybe if, like Maggie, I chose never to take another gander inside the bag, I could label the weirdness of the day before as an isolated event — a one-time thing. And who knows, maybe it was. If my sense of time were correct, the last item to appear out of the bag, the steak, arrived just before midnight. And this was a new day.

What I was getting at was that maybe the magic did have something to do with yesterday — the specific day — Tuesday, the twentieth day of December. Something special about it where, unbeknownst to astronomers around the world, the planets aligned in a unique formation, a once-in-every-zillion-years phenomenon that for reasons beyond our human comprehension caused all antique luggage to act peculiarly. Maybe it had happened all over the world, and if I turned on the TV at that moment, there they'd be — from Moscow to Cairo to Duluth — ordinary people relating their extraordinary stories of how yesterday their old travel bags had produced wonderfully outrageous, yet necessary gifts for strangers.

Why not? I decided right then and there to buy into my preposterous theory and attempt to rationalize it by not opening the bag ever again.

From a carton of low-fat, Maggie poured milk into my cereal and planted a spoon in the mix. I walked over to the kitchen counter, sat down on a stool, and scooped a load of what tasted like sugarcoated Styrofoam into my mouth.

"After I drop the cats off down the hall, I can give you a lift to your car on my way to the airport if you'd like," Maggie said.

"That would be great, thanks. So are you traveling to Florida with anyone special?"

"No. Just me."

"You meeting anyone there?"

"Nope. Actually I take that back. I *am* going with someone." She walked over to a leather handbag lying on the bookshelf. "Someone who's charming, clever, insightful, and highly unpredictable." She pulled a big, shiny-jacketed book out of her purse and held it up. "And although he won't be rubbing suntan lotion all over my body, I'm hoping he'll be interesting enough company to hold my attention while I'm turning a golden brown." I wasn't sure whether to feel sorry for her or admire her independence. She tossed the book to me underhand, like a mom teaching her kid to play catch.

I didn't recognize the title or author but proceeded to open it and flip through the pages like I was looking for pictures. "I noticed your collection last night. Guess you like to read, huh?"

"I do. In fact I pretty much do it for a living. I work for a small publishing company proofreading and whatnot. But reading novels . . . to get totally lost inside a story . . . what could be better? I guess you could say it's my passion. And what's your passion, sir?"

I didn't answer her, and she was kind enough to let it slide, aware that I already felt like I'd revealed more of myself than a frog on its back in Biology 101.

The truth was I didn't *get* passion—the concept—and didn't know why. Certainly I'd been enthusiastic about things—my job, definitely about Kathy and the kids—but *passionate*? I wasn't sure. I'd seen passion in the eyes of basketball players driving for the bucket, heard it in the voice of Martin Luther King Jr., and read it in the words of old love letters from Kathy in the early days of our relationship. But for me to be consumed by something, to love it so much that I'd feel desperate without it was an elusive sensation.

Van Gogh—I'd always thought of him as the definitive example of passion. It was supposed to be apparent in his paintings, in his letters to his brother, Theo, in his arguments with Gauguin. Vincent was so consumed with the need to express himself that he'd rather have died than not paint. And it wasn't just his work; it was his life, his "lust for life" as they say. And this passion carried over to his relationships. He became so overwrought about a quarrel with his friend Gauguin that he cut off a part of his ear. Insanity I understood. It's passion that always baffled me.

At one point I thought I'd take a stab at being a fine artist, back before I ended up art directing for animation and developing characters for video games. I admit there was something fascinating to me about the idea of it. I envisioned myself with a goatee and beret, living up in some big, skylighted loft in Paris or Florence, surrounded by the smell of oils and turpentine, the sounds of Gregorian chants, and most of all, by my work— expressive art, paintings that exuded a restless soul striving to find itself. It sounded exciting, romantic, bohemian. So I bought a bunch of tubes of oils and began slopping paint on huge canvases to release some grand passion that was surely stirring within me. And it wasn't that I wasn't competent on some technical level, but when I put my brush to the canvas . . . nothing. No feelings of enthusiasm swelled up inside of me; nothing even stirred. I may as well have been painting the kitchen walls yellow.

As Maggie and I ate breakfast, we spoke of hurricanes and freeze-dried fruit and the Westminster Dog Show but never mentioned a word about the bag. It was as if it had been removed from our consciousness like algebra.

Packed and ready for her vacation, Maggie joined me outside under an overcast sky. It didn't feel like a Wednesday. In fact, I'd nearly forgotten that I even held a job. It felt like an eighth day, or like a snow day when I was a kid—I made the day up as I went along. Going to work was out of the question, so I called to let the office know I wouldn't be in.

Maggie dumped her brown tweed suitcase and matching travel bag into the back seat of her Saturn, and I hopped into the front, loosely holding onto the carpetbag. The temptation to look inside had subsided just as I had hoped. With her eyes on the road and her hands at ten and two, Maggie began humming along with the radio. This was the best mood I'd seen her in so far. And why not—her immediate future offered warmth, the excitement of unpredictability, and best of all, escape.

I wanted to avoid prognosticating about my future without Kathy. But I had a hunch I'd end up like one of those old geezers who walks around all day unaware that one of his shirttails or a booger was hanging out, and nobody bothers to tell him because it just wouldn't matter enough to either party. So I tried to concentrate on Maggie's happiness instead.

"So what are you going to do with your *friend* now?" Maggie asked.

"Probably put it back where I found it."

"I think that's an excellent idea," Maggie said brightly. "I'm sure the ghost of Houdini misses it terribly. And what about David—what are your plans for him?"

"I don't know."

"Maybe you should take a vacation yourself. Get out of town for a while. Get a new perspective on your life."

"No. I'd just be taking my troubles with me."

"You have any family back east—New York, maybe?" She looked at me.

"No. Why do you ask?"

"No reason. You're right. You should just spend Christmas in Chicago."

The lazy shadows of clouds that grayed the snow-covered fields to my right were becoming more defined among the shifting patches of filtered sunlight on the ground. Gradually the landscape transformed into a bright, dazzling scene, the sun deciding to make a showing for the first time in several days. Through my side window, I could feel the warmth of its rays on my cheek. Adjusting my seat back to recline, I closed my eyes and imagined that I was now sitting in a low-slung canvas chair on the sandy shores of a California beach. The low grind of the heater served as the sound of continuously crashing waves, and the humming belonged to Kathy, lying alongside me on a beach towel wearing her stupendous purple one-piece. It wasn't hard to imagine at all; it was like the pleasant vacation we had taken a few years earlier.

The sunshine on my cheek began to move across the front

of my face, penetrating my eyelids as I sensed Maggie making a right-hand turn. I reached up blindly and flipped my sunshade down, opened my eyes and there, walking in the crosswalk right in front of us, was an old man. "Maggie, look *out!*"

Maggie slammed on the brakes, sending us spinning past the man and across the opposite lane, just missing a van. Centrifugal force threw me against the passenger door where I grabbed the handle to brace myself for impact. A poor choice. As the car slid out of control, the weight of my body pushed against the door, sending it flying open with me still holding on. My upper body stretched halfway out of the car like something out of Looney Tunes, while my seat belt held the rest of me in. Maggie's side of the car crashed into a pile of plowed snow, snapping my torso back into the cabin. The door followed my lead and slammed shut.

I immediately replayed the surreal moment over and over in my head, the way TV news programs replay catastrophes caught on tape. The engine had died, leaving us in complete silence.

"You okay?" I asked her.

Visibly shaken, Maggie looked over at me like I was a madman. "What in the world was that about?"

"What do you mean?" I asked.

"Why did you yell at me?"

"Because I thought you were going to kill the guy if I didn't."

"What guy?"

"The old man in the middle of the crosswalk."

"What are you talking about? Nobody was in the crosswalk."

I looked out the window toward the crosswalk, but the man was nowhere to be seen.

"You could have gotten us killed! Or worse, I could have missed my vacation."

"I'm sorry. I swear I saw . . ." My confusion about the man was replaced by a brand new confusion. ". . . the bag. Where's the bag?" I briefly looked around the floor and over my shoulder into the backseat, but like the man in the crosswalk, it had disappeared.

"Hey."

I looked over at Maggie whose eyes were alert. She nodded as she stared past me out my window. I turned around and there, about ten feet away on top of a pile of snow lay the carpetbag, sunning itself like a gecko on a rock. Maggie and I both silently eyed the bag.

"Leave it," Maggie suggested. She threw the gearshift into park and turned the key. The engine didn't quite turn over.

She had a point. It would be easy enough to just move on, especially if she could get her car back on the road without either of us having to step outside to assist in the process. She could see I was still staring at it. "Really, David. It's a perfect opportunity." She tried one more approach. "It needs to be free." She smiled and tried the ignition again. This time the car started, and the radio came on, playing Dan Fogelberg's "Longer."

Now I've never been big on signs—never read anything into crop circles or the Virgin Mary's image showing up on a taco shell somewhere in Amarillo. Never saw it as anything more than a fluke when I had received a phone call out of the blue from an old friend or relative about whom I was thinking at that very moment. I'm a firm believer in coincidence and the law of averages, which implies that it's logical for very strange things to happen occasionally.

But when I looked again at the carpetbag sitting on that hill of snow, I noticed that right above and beyond the top arch formed by the bag were the words Roosevelt Elementary School written across the front of the old brick building. It was the school where Kathy taught. This had to be sign. This morning's dream wasn't just a dream, and this accident wasn't an accident, and that bag didn't simply leap out of the car in the direction of my wife for no reason. And why did the radio decide to play that Fogelberg song at that particular moment? It was the song that was drifting out of my Mustang's radio all those years ago when Kathy and I were parked by Cherry Orchard Lake making out and planning our life together — the song she'd proclaimed right then and there to be *our* song.

Just as Maggie shifted the car into gear, and we began moving forward, I opened the door and stepped outside.

"David, no." Maggie sighed.

I tramped through the snow, snatched the bag off the drift, and kept walking toward the school.

"Where are you going?" Maggie yelled.

"I'll be right back." I crossed the playground, trying not to think too much about what I was doing — how I'd crossed some invisible line of reason. The brass bar across the front door clanged as I pushed on it and entered the school.

Mine were the only footsteps to be heard, squeaking down the institutional green hallway tiles. I turned the corner, past a wall covered with large tempera paintings of zoo animals in primary colors, walked down the hall to room 106, and peered through the small window in the door.

Wearing a long red cardigan, Kathy was standing at the blackboard writing in broad chalk strokes. She couldn't have looked more attractive if she were wearing a fancy gown by one of those Italian designers. She looked so much at home in front of that class that I had second thoughts about interrupting her.

As Kathy spun around on her heels to face the class, she caught me out of the corner of her eye. Holding her hand up to the class to excuse herself, she walked over toward me, wearing an expression very different from the one in my dream. She opened the door and stepped halfway out, not ready to commit to a full visit. "David, what are you doing here?"

I wasn't sure. But then the words "Hi, Kathy, I have something for you" spilled out of my mouth.

"Now? Here? I'm in the middle of class."

"I think it might be important."

"Fine," Kathy said with sigh of resignation. "You've got about thirty seconds before the inmates begin to revolt." She slipped into the hallway, gently closing the door behind her. She folded her arms with a demeanor that challenged the importance of my visit. I wasn't positive I was up to that challenge, but I had little to lose except my last ounce of dignity. The carpetbag had served others well, the policeman and his wife, the man in the bar with the swelling eye. Maybe if *I* couldn't make Kathy happy, something in this bag could. And though I had no notion that anything was lurking inside the bag, I put my confidence in it just the same.

"It's a gift."

"Gifts are not the solution to our situation."

"I know, I know," I said. "But, please . . ." I held up the bag by its straps and spread it open in front of her. "Just take a look inside."

"You've been drinking, haven't you?"

"No."

"Where'd you dig this old thing up?"

"Please, just look inside." Kathy looked down into the bag, reached inside, and pulled out an object half-concealed in her hand. She opened up her fingers and there in her palm was an old carved wooden egg about the size of a chicken egg. The red paint that once coated the egg was almost completely worn off, revealing the smooth, wheat-colored grain.

The good news was that the bag was back open for business. The bad news was . . .

"It's an egg," I said objectively.

"You sound surprised." More than surprised, I was disappointed. Why would Kathy need a wooden egg? The weird thing was that, although I didn't recall ever seeing anything like it before, something about it felt familiar.

"It opens up," I said. Unimpressed, Kathy looked closer and found a middle seam. "Just give it a little twist."

Kathy did just that, splitting it open to reveal a blue wooden egg only slightly smaller and less worn than the first. I wasn't sure where this was leading, but I was counting on the old adage that good things come in small packages. The low buzz of children's voices began to seep out the door from the classroom. Letting out another sigh of frustration, Kathy shook the egg, aware of a third object inside. "I really don't have time for this game."

She quickly opened the second egg, exposing a third one, once again smaller, and its green exterior slightly less worn. "Is this fun for you, David? Because . . ."

It wasn't. It was painful. Scratchy, high-pitched voices began to build in volume on the other side of the door, adding to Kathy's impatience as she twisted open the third egg. It was made of solid wood, and carved into each side was the concave impression of a heart.

"So that's it? This is what was so important that you had to take me away from my class?"

"I guess," I said in a stupor.

"Is this supposed to be symbolic of something? Is that it?"

"No. Look, Kathy, I thought—"

"Then what's this all about?"

I searched my brain for a connection. "I'm not sure."

Sufficiently perturbed, Kathy began to hastily deposit her collection of wooden egg halves into the pockets of her sweater, as paper wads and hyperactive children flashed past the window behind her. "Well, when you find out, be sure to let me know, okay?" Opening the classroom door to chaos, she bravely took a step inside.

"Listen, you don't understand. It's this bag. There's something very—"

"Please!" Kathy turned around toward me, and at that moment, a paper airplane performed a perfect one-point landing, embedding itself in her hair. "This is not a good time," she said primly, turning on her heel and pulling the door closed behind her. I cursed the bag and heaved it down the hallway. It tumbled end over end several times but landed upright, waiting patiently for me to pick it up on the way out.

Maggie had already managed to maneuver the Saturn out of the drift and back onto the snowy shoulder as I approached the car. Out of the window she yelled, "It's about time."

"Sorry."

"I'm going to be late for my flight at this rate."

I got in the car. Feeling cheated and humiliated by the carpetbag, I crammed it down between my feet.

Maggie looked down at the bag. "For a second there I thought you were going off somewhere to trash that thing. Where'd you go anyway?"

"Kathy works at that school."

Maggie looked at me like it was no big deal, but I didn't buy it for a second. She had to be curious. But she remained stubbornly silent, stepped down on the accelerator, and we took off down the road.

"It's not dead after all," I finally said.

"As far as I'm concerned it is."

"Yesterday you were all jazzed about the bag. What—"

"That was yesterday."

"You've got to hear this, Maggie—"

She held up her hand. "No."

"But it doesn't make any sense at all," I continued. "I showed Kathy the bag, and you know what came out of it?"

In an auctioneer's delivery she proclaimed, "I don't wanna know; I don't wanna hear; I don't wanna know."

"But I need to tell you."

"No, that's where you're wrong. You don't need to tell me anything. And do you know why? 'Cause I just don't care. I am without care. I am going on vacation to the land of sunshine and pink flamingos, and hopefully never seeing you or your ludicrous bag again. No offense."

I looked out the window at the big white cumulus clouds climbing on top of each other in front of a saturated blue sky. "It was a wooden egg." I felt compelled to say it.

"Fine! So he tells me anyway." She shook her head.

"Actually it was a series of wooden eggs, one inside the next, and in the middle—"

"I don't want to hear this."

"The thing is, I vaguely remember something like that before —a long time ago."

"Really, David, stop. It's all just too creepy."

She was right about that. Creepy and senseless—not a good combination. Kathy had no desire, much less need, for a dumb knickknack. I was sure of that. I'd obviously overestimated the power of the bag. I kept my mouth shut for the next few minutes until I spotted my car up ahead at the curb. Right where the big cop had left it. "This is me right up here. The Volvo."

Maggie pulled up behind my car. "I really appreciate the ride," I said. "Have a great time in Florida. And I'm sorry I dragged you into all of this. I just can't help wondering what it all means."

Maggie held out her hand. "It means it was nice meeting you, and I'll be leaving the twilight zone now, thank you." Then she leaned in close and whispered ominously, "Destroy it before it destroys you."

As I opened the car door, Maggie stopped me with a touch on the arm and said, "Listen, I'm sorry I called you a pholeaziat. You're not. In fact, you're quite the contrary. And I hope somehow you and Kathy"—Maggie's mobile phone began to ring—"manage to work things out."

She picked up the receiver from its cradle between the two seats. "Hello . . . yes, this is she. Oh, yes, of course I do."

Not a fan of long good-byes, I found this to be a good time to exit, stage right.

"Yes, well," she went on, "definitely, I'm still interested."

I gave Maggie a wave and closed the door. Though preoccupied, she managed to acknowledge my gesture with a smile. I walked over to my car, snatched a new parking ticket from underneath my windshield wiper, and stashed it in my coat pocket. I opened the car door, tossed the carpetbag onto the passenger seat, and sat myself down behind the wheel to consider my next step.

Just as I decided to revert back to plan A—to take the bag back up to the roof—I heard a car door slam behind me.

I looked in my side-view mirror, and there was Maggie standing alongside her car, frantically waving her arms around in the air like she was being attacked by killer bees. I dashed out of my car and ran back to her.

"You all right? What's going on?"

"Aaaahhh! Shoot! This is just so—I can't believe it." She continued to flail.

"What is it that you can't believe?"

"Stockton Press. It's this publishing company in New York that I've been trying to get a job with for the longest time. They have an opening for an assistant editor. It's an unbelievable opportunity."

"So what's the problem?"

"They want to fill the spot before the holidays, so they asked me if I could come in and interview on Thursday. Tomorrow."

"What did you tell them?"

"I told them 'fine.'"

"You're upset because you're going to miss your vacation?" I asked.

"No. I can still go down to Florida after the interview. Blast it."

"So I don't get it. You should be happy."

Maggie reached into her coat pocket and pulled out a slip of paper, looked at it for a moment, and then reluctantly handed it to me, like a young girl turning over a lousy report card to her father.

It took me a few seconds to realize what it was: a train ticket. "So?"

"Shoot! I was so sure it was meant for you," she said.

I looked the ticket over again. "What are you talking about?

It's just a train ticket . . . departing Chicago . . . arriving in New York . . . leaving December twenty-first. That's today. Where'd you get this?"

Maggie folded her arms across the curved roof of the Saturn and rested her forehead up against them.

"Where do you think?"

"You're kidding. You said you didn't look inside."

"So I lied—sue me." Maggie unfolded her arms and stood up straight. "I couldn't help myself. It was a sanity check. When I found the ticket this morning, I figured I'd do you a favor and not tell you about it. You know, help you end this obsession. How did it know, David?" She looked at me pleadingly. "This is not my bag. This shouldn't be my nightmare."

"What nightmare? You would never have been able to get a flight out today. It gave you what you needed—a chance at your dream job. Consider it another gift."

"Yeah, well, call me old-fashioned, but I believe gifts should be given by people, not luggage."

"Maybe it is from someone. Maybe it's from J. O. E. Could be that he's a lonely old poltergeist in need of a traveling companion."

"Oh, thank you—like I needed that additional chill down my spine. I'll take the ticket, but you keep that bag away from me."

I handed the ticket back to her, and she took a closer look at both sides of it. "How do we even know if it's any good?" she asked.

six

PEOPLE
GET READY . . .

Beneath an immense, arching concrete ceiling, I stood anxiously on the platform at the train station, the carpetbag at my side. I was waiting for Maggie to come down from the ticket counter while passengers boarded the growling mechanical dinosaur before me. Train stations had always struck me as the most ironic of locations. Vast and impersonal, yet they provided such intimate moments for people. Train stations could conjure up images of heartfelt reunions involving lovers or friends or family. But for me, they represented only departure and separation.

I hadn't actually visited many train stations in my lifetime, so maybe the feeling of melancholy that began to wrap me up came from watching old black-and-white movies on TV. Some handsome guy with a stiff upper lip was always traveling off somewhere, usually to war. Leaning out the window as the train slowly chugged away from the depot, he'd be waving to his best girl while she waded in a sea of steam, tears rolling down her cheeks, her heaving breast encasing a heart breaking with the anticipation of loneliness. Or maybe the sadness I was experiencing was from something else entirely.

I missed Kathy. She had always helped define me — she'd been my magic mirror. And even though in recent years my reflection shone in a less than desirable light, at least I still had an identity. But my living alone had taken a toll in that respect; with no one there in that apartment, I'd felt myself fading away. I barely knew Maggie, but now she, too, was leaving.

A veteran conductor, long gray hair spilling out from under his blue cap, was pacing back and forth in front of the hissing passenger train, calling out in a deep, gravelly voice, "All aboard. All aboard. Final call. All aboard." Passengers were saying their good-byes and scurrying aboard the train.

Maggie danced down the long flight of stairs, carrying a suit-case and her carry-on bag. Holding the ticket in her hand, she rushed up to me. "They thought I was a little crazy to ask, but apparently the ticket's perfectly good," she said. She remained standing directly in front of me, uncomfortably close.

"Well, have a nice trip," I said, "and best of luck with the interview."

Maggie dropped her bags and gave me an unexpected hug and kiss on the cheek. I slowly wrapped my arms around her in return. It had been a long time since I held someone like that. It felt odd but good. "Try to have a Merry Christmas, okay?" she whispered in my ear. "And I hope you find your way onto the stage."

"All aboard!" the conductor said with more conviction.

Maggie abruptly broke from the embrace, picked up her bags, scuttled off past the conductor, and boarded the train. Through the series of train windows, I watched her inch her way, left to right, through the crowded car until I lost sight of her.

When I was ready to leave, I reached down to pick up the carpetbag, but instead I found myself grabbing the handle of Maggie's tweed carry-on bag. The carpetbag was gone. She had picked up the wrong bag. Or had she? I was almost positive I hadn't seen Maggie carry it away, but I was pretty sure she had it. With her bag in hand, I ran over to the train and hopped on.

The aisle overflowed with passengers choosing seats and stashing their luggage in the overhead racks. "Tickets, tickets," the conductor requested from the middle of the aisle in front of me.

I tried to maneuver my way through the crowd. "Maggie! Maggie!" I called out, squishing my way down the aisle, unable to locate her anywhere in the car.

My path was blocked by the wide rear end of the conductor. I assumed he was the same conductor I'd seen outside, but as he turned around toward me, I saw that this was a middle-aged black man with gold wire-rimmed glasses. Charlie Jefferson—as his name tag read—held a punch in his hand, calling for, "Tickets . . . ticket, sir?"

"I don't have a ticket. Excuse me." The train gave a subtle lurch forward as I tried frantically to pass the conductor, but he stopped me with a shifting hip and a hand on my midsection. "Well, I'm sorry," he said, "but you can't ride the rails without a ticket."

"You don't understand," I said. "I'm just trying to return this bag to someone. I'm not traveling myself."

"Really? The scenery outside seems to suggest the contrary."

I looked out the window to see the station moving past and picking up speed. I panicked. "I need to get off this train!"

"Maybe you just misplaced your ticket, sir," Charlie suggested strangely, with a pleasant smile.

"No, I don't have a ticket."

Just then, Maggie entered the far end of the car, eyes bugging out, carrying the carpetbag with her arms extended in front of her as if the bag were about to explode.

"Maggie!"

She spotted me standing in the middle of the car with the conductor. "David!" She plowed through several people in the aisle, bowling a couple of them down like she was converting a baby split, and then rushed toward me with her time bomb.

"It's possessed. Get this thing out of my life before it spits out a toe tag with my name on it." Maggie jammed the bag into my chest, collapsing its sides. A slip of paper immediately popped halfway out of the top of the bag, right under the conductor's wire-rims, startling Maggie. "Aaahhh!"

"Oh, there's your ticket, sir," Charlie said as he removed the train ticket from the top of the bag, punched it, and handed it over to me. "Do have a pleasant trip." He tipped his hat and continued down the aisle. "Tickets . . . tickets please."

Maggie took her tweed bag from my hand. A peculiar calm came over her face as she looked into my eyes and said, "Welcome aboard the train to hell."

I sat at the window seat and Maggie next to me, the carpetbag resting in the overhead bin above the seats opposite us, where we could keep an eye on it. Our seats were facing a twitchy-eyed woman with short, straight, jet black hair, knitting something maroon that had a better-than-average chance of becoming a scarf. She had introduced herself as Arlene Pickett. Maggie introduced us as business partners.

Arlene's six-year-old son, Ethan, sat beside her in the window seat. Apparently in need of an additional dose of Ritalin, Ethan was getting on his mom's nerves, pretending his hand was a fighter plane and accompanying his flight with impressive jet sounds that sprayed from his vibrating lips. As he was dive-bombing his hand on a round-trip run from alongside the windowpane to just below his mother's nose, it was easy to see why Arlene looked like she was on the verge of converting one of those knitting needles into a weapon. "*Varrooom . . . varrooom,*" Ethan roared.

"Ethan! Stop!" she'd say every so often. "Stop bothering the people." Each time, Ethan would shorten his flight pattern and knock down the jet sounds a few decibels for a couple of seconds before building them up all over again.

"I just want you to know," I said to Maggie, "I'm getting off at the next stop."

She began to laugh, a little chuckle at first, building to one of those hideous dramatic laughs that borders on comedic madness.

Intrigued by Maggie's behavior, Ethan landed his hand in his lap and gazed over at Maggie. Arlene stopped mid stitch to join him. Embarrassed, I quietly asked Maggie, "What's so amusing?" hoping she wouldn't share her answer with our neighbors.

"You think that bag up there is predicting our future, don't you?" Maggie said loudly.

"*Shhh.* Yeah, maybe," I said. "So?"

"I got news for you, buddy. It's *planning* our future."

"What are you talking about?" I asked.

"You're only getting off this train if old Mr. Carpetbag up there thinks it's a good idea," Maggie said, extending her finger alongside her nose, taking aim at the carpetbag above.

Ethan eyed the bag and belly laughed at Maggie.

"See, he knows," Maggie said, grinning like a cartoon cat who'd just been bopped over the head with a large mallet. "He knows what I'm talking about."

Maggie's odd behavior was too much for Arlene Pickett, who squeezed her eyes down to disapproving slits and snatched up her big knit purse off the floor. She grabbed Ethan by his airplane hand, yanked him out of his seat, and dragged him down the aisle in search of saner traveling companions. I was about to search for one myself.

"You're beginning to frighten me, Maggie."

"I am? In what way?"

"In the *Psycho* way."

"Yeah, well, apparently I get that way when luggage takes *me* on a trip instead of the other way around."

"Come the next stop, I'm gone," I promised her. "And I'm taking the bag with me."

"Don't I wish."

I turned away from Maggie and looked out the window. Between the old tenement buildings, I could see the Chicago skyline beginning to shrink. We entered a tunnel and everything went dark. I don't remember feeling particularly tired or my eyelids shutting and my brain drifting off to dreamland, but there it was.

A long-legged figure in yellow Bermuda shorts is bounding ahead of me, blurred with motion. Chasing the person through seas of long summer grass swaying in the breeze, as fast as I can run, but I can't catch up. Sounds of giggling and a barking dog. Long branches of a huge oak tree stretch out in all directions around me. Holding something in my hands . . . a box . . . a black box. Long blonde hair worn in a ponytail, flashing, dancing ahead of me. I try to catch up. The figure darts, zigs, zags, and finally dashes behind a tree to hide. Slowly, I hold the box up, and approach the tree with caution. . . . A Raggedy Ann doll leaps out at me from behind the tree. "Noooo!"

I bolted awake in my train seat, startling Maggie.

"Are you all right?"

"Yeah . . . fine." I took a deep breath. "I guess I fell asleep. Boy, I was just having this weird dream."

"What about?"

Several new passengers walking down the aisle caught my attention. "Hey, did we stop?"

"Maybe," Maggie said in a playfully coy voice, turning away.

"Why didn't you wake me?"

"What, and ruin my bag theory?"

"Where are we anyhow?" I looked out the window at the snow falling. I turned to Maggie. "You don't understand. I need to get off this train. I want to go home."

Charlie the conductor happened to be walking by at that moment, and I reached my hand out to stop him. "Excuse me. Could you tell me where we are?" My fear was that he was going to announce, "Willoughby, next stop Willoughby." But instead he said something equally strange.

"The best part about traveling on a train, young man, is not having to worry about time—where you're at or when you'll arrive. The important thing is to know that you'll always reach your destination right on schedule." He smiled and continued down the aisle.

"Was that not just a little peculiar?" I asked Maggie.

Totally ignoring my question, Maggie asked, "So what was going on in that dream of yours?"

"Nothing. And you're changing the subject."

"Not necessarily," she said. "Honestly—what startled you like that?"

"I don't know. I was just running . . . being chased or something."

"By whom? Where?"

"I don't know." She stared me down for an answer. "Okay, there was a field, and then there were these trees."

"Trees?"

"Actually just one tree. And I was holding something . . . I think it was a box of some sort."

"A box?" she asked, sounding way too intrigued. "What kind of box?"

"Is this really important to you?"

"Exceedingly."

"It was sort of small, about yea-big." With my hands I measured out a size comparable to a head of lettuce. "It was black, I think."

"And who was chasing you?"

I started to remember more details of the dream. "Nobody. I mean I was the one doing the chasing."

"You were chasing after somebody? That doesn't sound very frightening. Who was it?"

"I have no idea. I never saw the person's face. And then she hid behind the tree. And there was this dog—"

"A dog—a dog scared you?"

"No."

"So what scared you?"

Just then it came back to me, but I thought it best to keep it to myself. "I don't know."

"Oh, come on. You must remember."

"No, I don't."

"Come on!" she said. "It just frightened the heck out of you a minute ago. What *was* it?"

"Fine," I said, knowing she wouldn't let it die. "It was . . ." *Maybe she won't laugh.* "It was . . ." *Maybe she'd understand that it was just an abstract, meaningless dream, and not laugh.* "It was . . . Raggedy Ann."

Maggie let loose with a loud and hearty laugh that turned several heads in our direction. "Raggedy Ann? As in the doll? Terrifying, impoverished, red-headed?"

"Hey, she lunged out at me from behind a tree!"

"Well, maybe you shouldn't have been chasing her with a stupid box! You're lucky she didn't sic her big brother Andy on you."

"It was just a dream. I can't be held responsible for what I dream."

Just then a young man in an Army uniform stopped in the aisle beside Maggie. "Excuse me. Are either of these seats taken?" He gestured to the seats evacuated by Ethan and his mom.

"No. Help yourself," Maggie said.

"Thank you, ma'am." The soldier lofted his duffle bag up into the overhead rack across the aisle, nudging the carpetbag closer to the edge. Maggie began to fidget in her seat. The young man removed his coat, tossed it onto the window seat, and sat down across from Maggie. He looked out the window, removed his cap, and knocked the snow off the top of it. "Boy it's snowing like a madman out there."

"Going home for Christmas?" Maggie asked.

"Yes, ma'am. Just finished up boot camp, and I'm going home to Glenview, Ohio."

"Oh yeah? I grew up in Glenview," I said.

"Is that right, sir?"

"Yeah. My name's David, and this is Maggie," I said, shaking his hand.

"Nice to meet you both. My name's Peter."

"My family lived out in the northwest end of town near the

water tower," I said. "But I couldn't have been more than eight when we moved away. I probably wouldn't recognize the place now."

"Oh, I don't know," Peter said. "I can't imagine that it's changed that much. It still has that small town — "

Suddenly an object fell from the overhead compartment, landing at the soldier's feet. "Whoa," Peter exclaimed. He bent over and picked up a metallic, rectangular black box off the floor and looked it over. Maggie's eyes met mine. "Where the heck did this thing come from?" he asked.

Maggie and I looked up at the carpetbag now lying on its side at the edge of the overhead compartment, its top wide open. "Must have fallen out of the bag," I said.

"What is this, anyway?" Peter asked, rotating the box in his hands.

"It's a box — a black one at that," Maggie informed him as she looked my way again.

It was more than just a box. In fact, I knew exactly what it was. "Actually it's a camera — a box camera," I said.

Upon further inspection, Peter said, "Oh, right. Here's the lens. It's pretty old, huh?" He handed me the camera.

I began to remember. "My dad had one just like this . . . gave it to me when he bought his Polaroid."

"*Reeeally*," Maggie said.

"I remember taking pictures of friends. It made me feel grown up."

"You were trying to take a picture," Maggie said softly to me. "What?"

"In the dream, the person you were chasing — you were trying to take her picture."

I thought about it for a moment and realized she was right.

This was the box that I had been holding in my dream.

Peter looked up at the bag, then at me. "The bag belongs to you?"

"Yes," Maggie said, "it's most definitely David's bag. So Peter . . . is there any reason you might want this camera?"

Peter looked understandably puzzled by the question. "No, ma'am. I don't believe so."

I couldn't find the sense in it, like the case of the mysterious wooden eggs. Maybe the bag was confused.

"But I could use a decent picture of myself in uniform to give to my girl back home," Peter added.

"Ah, you have a girlfriend?" Maggie asked.

"Yes, ma'am. Laura—the sweetest, prettiest girl in Glenview. Can't wait to see her."

Maggie folded her arms. "And this Laura, she's pretty delighted that you're in the service?" There was a slight edge to her voice.

"Well, honestly, no. I mean, she knows how I feel about serving my country."

"And how's that?" Maggie asked.

"Proud. Privileged. But I know Laura worries about me . . . misses me."

"And still you decided to enlist?" Maggie leaned forward, putting him on the defensive.

"I'm not sure what you mean, ma'am."

"I don't know if this antique still works, but I'll be happy to try to take your photo," I said, trying to run interference.

"Thank you, sir. I'd appreciate that." Peter turned his attention back to Maggie. "You see, ma'am—"

"Could you please stop calling me ma'am?" Maggie said. "It makes me feel just this side of ancient."

"Oh, I am sorry. I was just going to say that I never really thought much about joining the service. And then with all the stuff that's been going on . . . innocent people dying . . . I couldn't just sit back and hope the bad guys would just go away on their own. But I have to admit my duty hasn't been quite as exciting as those commercials you see on TV—the ones with all the helicopters flying in low, the tanks barreling across the fields, paratroopers jumping out of planes, and American flags waving everywhere like it was the Fourth of July . . . they make it seem pretty darn thrilling." Peter was starting to sound like he'd just stepped out of a Norman Rockwell illustration. "You've seen those, haven't you, ma'am?"

Maggie clearly couldn't help herself. "Yeah, I have. I especially like the ones that show all the boys coming back from combat in body bags. I find those very engaging."

"Ma'am?" he asked, looking puzzled.

"I'm also partial to those other ones—" Maggie began.

"Maggie, don't," I said.

But she was deaf to interference. "The ones that show the bloodied soldiers lying in the battlefields with body parts blown off, or the shots of the mothers and fathers standing over their sons' graves."

I looked down at the counter on the camera. "Maggie . . . *Maggie.*"

"What?" she asked impatiently.

"Well, I just noticed that the picture counter is only on number one. So there should be an entire roll of film in here already."

"That's perfect," said Maggie. "You go ahead—*Peter*. You take your little portrait shot for your honey. Take as many as you like. I'm sure they'll be of great comfort to her if, God forbid, you should ever see combat, and she should get a call . . ." Maggie covered her face for a moment.

"Ma'am, you all right?" Unable to stop the flow of emotion, she suddenly stood up and rushed down the aisle.

"Maggie!" I called out, but she kept going.

"I'm sorry," Peter said to me. "Was it something I said?"

"No. It had nothing to do with you." I raised the camera to my eye and framed up Peter through the small lens. "Ready? Look heroic."

Peter forced a smile, and I snapped the photo.

seven

EVERY PICTURE
TELLS A STORY

The fat dining car door rolled closed behind me, slamming out the roar of wind and wheels. Air thick with the aroma of greasy chicken rushed through my nostrils and down the back of my throat, settling on my tongue. I tracked Maggie down to a two-seater window booth, where she was nursing a beer and staring out at the passing countryside. I set the carpetbag down on the gray Formica table.

"Are you okay?" I asked.

Maggie took her time finishing up a sip from her glass. "You still here? I thought you and your bag buddy there would have jumped train by now." Though I could tell she was in no mood for company, she nodded permission for me to sit. I slid onto the springy cushioned seat and set the bag next to me on the floor. "Why are you so anxious to go home, anyway? Sounded like you already managed to send that bridge up in flames." She shot an apologetic glance my way. "Sorry, that wasn't fair."

Maybe Maggie knew what she was talking about. Could be

I was supposed to be on that train. With all my ranting about wanting to go home, it was true that I had no real home to go back to anymore. Maybe riding a train in the dead of winter with no destination was the most appropriate place for me to be. "No, you're right—home will never again be what it used to be. Or maybe it never even *was* what it used to be."

"So what kind of place would you like it to be?"

"Home?"

"Yeah, home. In twenty words or less."

"Oh, I don't know . . . easy . . . safe . . . simple, I suppose. A place where I could scream out at the top of my lungs and everyone would understand why. Genuine . . . comfortable . . . restful, a place where I could feel like I belonged. Like I was part of the puzzle. Maybe most of all, a place where I could be forgiven."

"Forgiven? For what?"

"I don't know. I guess for all the things I am . . . and all the things I'm not."

"That's a lot of things." Maggie smiled at me in a sad kind of way.

"I went over my twenty-word limit, didn't I?"

"It's okay. I didn't notice."

"And what would *home* mean to you?" I asked.

"I'm not good at answering hypothetical questions, just asking them."

I opened up the carpetbag and looked inside. "I thought maybe it would go back to where it came from." Maggie looked bewildered until I reached into the bag, pulled out the box camera, and placed it on the table.

Maggie picked it up and began examining it. "And where do you think that is?"

"Who knows?"

"You said you remembered the wooden egg from somewhere."

"It seemed familiar."

"And now this camera—you said you had one just like it as a kid. There has to be a connection, don't you think?"

A waiter led Ethan and his mom, Arlene, to the vacant table across the aisle from us. When Arlene noticed us, she asked the waiter, "You have no other tables available?" It was obvious that there were none.

"Not at the moment, ma'am," he replied. Arlene reluctantly sat down; her son sat across from her. She wouldn't look at us, but Ethan gave us a little wave, which we returned.

The waiter turned to us. "Would you like to order?"

I picked up the menu. "Did you want to get something to eat?" I asked Maggie.

"Yeah, I could probably go for something."

"If you could give us a minute, thanks." The waiter nodded, turned, and walked off.

While I perused the menu, Maggie held the camera up close to her face. "Wow," she said.

"What is it?" I asked.

"This camera . . . the counter was at one before you took Peter's photo, right?"

"Yeah?"

"So now it's showing zero. These old cameras counted *down* as pictures were taken." She handed me the camera to check it out.

"So you're saying it's out of pictures?"

"Well, yes, but more importantly, I'm saying that there were at least nine pictures already in this camera."

I looked over at Ethan. He slowly started up his jet plane routine again. This time a bread stick served as his airplane of choice.

"Aren't you the least bit curious about what might be on that film?" Maggie asked.

Maybe I should have been, but there was something about Ethan that was holding my attention—his fascination with flight. A fascination I'd also held as a kid. I remembered lying on my back on the blue tiled roof of our house, watching jet planes scream across the sky until they ran out of breath. They'd sail out of sight, leaving behind that white line that looked like chalk across the blackboard. A line that would magically disappear in minutes.

"Ethan, your food is to be eaten, not flown," his mom informed him. He looked over at me for a moment.

"You like airplanes?" I asked him.

He nodded without speaking.

"Me, too,"

"David, are you listening to anything I'm saying?" Maggie asked.

Arlene seized the breadstick out of Ethan's hand to end the mission. His attention was drawn to the bag that sat on the floor between us. I lifted the bag onto the cushion beside me.

"Want to see what's inside?" I asked.

"Are you sure that's a good idea?" Maggie said.

"I don't know if there's anything in here, but you're welcome to look. Do you want to look?"

Ethan responded with an almost inaudible yes. I slid the bag closer to the boy as he began to get down off his chair.

"Ethan, what are you doing?" his mom said. Crossing the aisle, Ethan leaned over the bag. "Get back over here, young man. Leave that alone, Ethan."

Standing in the aisle, Ethan slowly spread open the top of the carpetbag. He extended his neck over the bag and peered curiously down into it. A wide smile broke across his face, and he pulled out a toy airplane, the kind that could be propelled by a rubber band beneath its thin balsa-wood body.

"Oh, my gosh," Maggie said. "It knew."

Ethan looked at me with uncertainty.

"Go ahead; it's yours," I said.

Ethan's face beamed with delight, though his mom's reaction was somewhat less enthusiastic. "Ethan . . ." she warned. He glanced in her direction. Her eyes were twitching like crazy.

Ethan lifted the glider up to his face and gently flicked the red plastic propeller, spinning it back and forth. His eyebrows rose above his mischievous blue eyes as he slowly raised the plane with one hand above his head. He looked over at his mom one last time and then . . . took off ("*Neeeoow!*") running through the dining car, dive-bombing patrons' heads, and swerving past a waiter with a trayful of food.

Ethan's mom glared over at me with a look that could kill, but it didn't faze me. I had given the boy what he needed.

I felt Maggie's hand touch mine. "You're starting to enjoy this gig, aren't you?"

And at least for the moment, I was.

eight

THE TRUTH ABOUT CATS AND DOGS

Pacifying the dozing passengers with its gentle side-to-side rocking motion and the lullaby of its muffled, rhythmic *clickity-clack*, the train car was peaceful as we traveled into the night. I'd removed the carpetbag from the overhead compartment and stashed it safely under my seat, just in case someone in desperate need of a bowling ball walked by.

Snowflakes appearing out of the darkness silently crashed against the window, melting into watery veins and spreading out into windblown capillaries.

Reclined in her seat, Maggie rested with her eyes closed, her blanket tucked high under her chin. Her exposed boots extended onto the empty seats across from us. She stirred and said sleepily, "Seems we aren't very good company."

I was about to point out that she was the one responsible for scaring off Arlene, Ethan, and Peter, but with her eyes still closed, she beat me to it. "Check that," she murmured. "*I'm* the one who chased them all away."

I agreed completely, but felt I should be sympathetic. "Why do you say that?"

"'Cause I chase everyone away. It's what I do. It's who I am. It's what I'm good at," she said with a yawn. She opened her eyes, squinting up at me. "There is an advantage to my talent, though."

"Really? And what would that be?"

"Foot room. Elbow room. Breathing room," she said.

"Do you really need that much room?"

She turned her body toward me. "You know that old song, 'People'? Barbra Streisand?"

"Yeah."

"So you think it's true what it says about people?" she asked.

"I don't know. I never really gave it much thought."

"Well, personally, I think ol' Babs got it all wrong. People who *don't* need people . . . we're the lucky ones."

"You're saying you didn't need Roger?"

"Roger?" She twisted the end of the blanket back and forth between her fingers. "I was just a kid back then. Roger existed in a whole different life for me—a past life. It's almost as if he never existed."

"He seemed pretty real when Peter joined us." Maggie got real quiet. It was none of my business, and I wished I had just kept my mouth shut.

"I'm just not a fan of man's inhumanity toward man," she said at last.

I wasn't sure which one of us she was trying to fool. "You know why I don't like cats?" I asked.

"What?"

"Cats. You asked me why I didn't like them."

"Yeah, about a year ago."

"Because you take a dog and you yell at him, scold him for doing something wrong, reject him in some way, and he'll stay by your side, cowering, looking up at you with sad eyes, whimpering, begging for forgiveness. But you do the same thing to a cat, and she struts off like she doesn't give a flying leap."

"So you don't like cats because they have high self-esteem — because they take criticism well?"

"No, that's not it," I said. "You see, I believe that when a cat gets bawled out for something and struts away, I think that cat actually goes somewhere private, away from everybody . . . where she breaks down and cries her heart out. I don't like cats because they won't admit that they hurt; they don't admit that they care."

Maggie looked at me like she might want to refute the analogy, but instead just turned away. I faced the window and caught my reflection staring back at me. I'd always thought that I looked more like my dad than my mom, but for the first time, I realized that I had my mom's eyes — large and round and unreadable.

"Did you ever feel like you were being punished by Roger's death?"

Maggie pulled her legs over to her chair and in tight to her body, adjusting the blanket around them.

"What do you mean?" she asked.

"My mom died when I was little. . . ."

"Really? I'm sorry. That must have been tough. Is that when you moved away — from Glenview, I mean?"

"No, we moved before that. But the point is I remember that when she died, I felt like I was being punished for something I had done."

"Like you were responsible?"

"No," I said, "more like I had done something to deserve

having my mom taken away from me. Something bad."

"So you felt like you were being punished by God?"

"I don't know. Maybe. You didn't feel that way when Roger died?"

Maggie looked straight ahead. "Sometimes bad things just happen." She paused, then turned toward me again. "Your dad raised you?"

"Yeah, me and my older brother and sister."

"Did you get along with him—your dad?"

"I suppose. I mean, he did things for me—took me to ball games and played catch with me, and all. . . . But after my mom died, I don't know; he didn't act the same toward me. We didn't talk as much. And I remember whenever he did talk to me, he'd always have his hand in his pocket. He always carried a pocketful of change on him, and he'd jingle it around with his hand the whole time he talked to me. I felt like if he didn't have that money in his pocket, he would never have been able to say a word to me."

"Do you ever think she's looking down on you?" Maggie asked.

"My mom? From heaven?"

"Yeah."

"It's funny. When she knew she was dying, she told me that even if God were to take her, she'd always be watching over me, wishing the best for me. But I've never had the slightest sense that my mom was looking down on me . . . much less anyone else. Hopefully, she's got better things to do."

Maggie didn't say anything for a long time, and then she laid her head against my shoulder. Her hair smelled sweet, almost like lemonade. It was nice just to have her lean up against me like that. I looked out the window and noticed that the snow had stopped falling. The moment filled me with an unfamiliar feeling—a tranquility that had escaped me for the longest time.

Without warning the train car lurched violently, jolting Maggie and me face-first into the seats across from us. From beneath us came a terribly shrill sound, like the relentless shrieks of a prehistoric beast. Screams filled the cabin as luggage flew from overhead carriages into the aisle and down upon jostled passengers. Maggie and I jerked backward as the wheels finally ground to a complete stop. The small cry of a child and a variety of moans could be heard around us. I grabbed Maggie by the shoulder and turned her around toward me. "Are you all right?"

"Yeah, I'm fine. What was that all about?"

The rude awakening turned to confusion. Strangers thrown into a situation of necessity turned to other passengers for physical assistance and emotional support. For the most part bumps and bruises were the extent of injuries in our area, with the occasional bloody lip.

Looking out my window, I noticed Charlie the conductor standing beside the train, surrounded by several passengers.

"I'm going to see what's up."

"I'm coming with you," Maggie said.

I slid the carpetbag farther under my seat. We navigated the crowded aisle and stepped off the train into the snow. The falling snow had subsided as clouds above us parted to reveal a pale blue, nearly full moon. The distant lights of a town ahead of us were the only signs of civilization for miles.

"Now there's no need for alarm," Charlie began. "We've already alerted the closest hospitals, and they'll be sending out ambulances to tend to any of the injured."

A woman in a big fur coat asked, "But what happened?"

A round man chimed in, "Yeah, why did we stop like that?"

"Well, if you look toward the front of the train," Charlie began, pointing in that direction, "you'll notice a pile of snow about thirty feet high covering the tracks. It was our carefully calculated decision not to bury ourselves in it."

"But where'd it all come from?" Maggie asked.

"Near as I can figure," Charlie said, "it was caused by an avalanche."

I looked around the bleak, only slightly hilly terrain, and said, "But there's not a mountain in sight."

Readjusting the cap to sit slightly askew on top of his head, Charlie turned around and looked directly at me and said, "Peculiar, ain't it? In fact, had I not seen it with my own eyes, I would not have believed it." Then, maybe it was my imagination, but I swear he gave me a wink before turning back around to face the rest of the group. It was real enough to send a shiver down the back of my neck. "So, as you may have guessed, we will not be moving any time soon," he continued. "You have a choice here. You can stay with the train, or if you're adventurous, you can begin hiking to that little town up ahead and bed down for the night. Either way, we'll keep you posted on our progress. We do apologize for the inconvenience."

Maggie and I climbed back aboard the train and began walking down the now less-congested aisle toward our seats, past passengers who appeared more composed at this juncture.

"This is just perfect," Maggie said. "He's messing with our minds; you know that, don't you?"

"Who, the conductor?"

Maggie plopped herself down in her seat.

"No."

"Who then?"

Maggie yanked the carpetbag up off the floor by its leather straps, dropped it on the seat across from her, and looked up at me.

"The bag?" I asked. "You think the bag is responsible for this?" I had to laugh.

"He lied to me. He played me for a fool."

"What are you talking about?"

"I'm not going to New York."

"You might still make it in time."

"It's not what he has in mind."

I refused to believe I didn't have a say in the matter of where my footsteps were headed. "So what do you want to do?" I asked her. "You want to crash here or start walking? We have a choice you know. It's not up to that stupid bag. It's our choice."

"If we're going to be spending the night without making any progress, we might as well be comfortable."

So we grabbed Maggie's luggage and the carpetbag and decided on the adventurous route, leaving the train behind.

We trudged through the snow, passed the enormous snow pile lit up by the engine's beam, and followed the railroad tracks toward the sprinkling of lights that was the town ahead of us. "Did you see how that conductor looked at me?" I asked Maggie.

"What are you talking about?"

"That comment about not believing it if he hadn't seen it with his own eyes."

"So what about it?"

I had a feeling she wouldn't understand. "Nothing. Never mind." But it was as if Charlie had listened in on my conversation with Pastor Neal and was letting me know it. It seemed crazy, but this *was* the same guy who never questioned my train ticket suddenly popping out of the top of the carpetbag.

"Florida," Maggie said, nearly out of breath. "It seemed like such a good idea."

DEERLY BELOVED . . .

M aggie and I crossed a snow-covered field, hopped a short
wire fence, and followed a two-lane road a half mile into
a rural town thick with pine trees. As we cut through a closed
Texaco gas station, we could see that the business district appeared
to comprise only a couple dozen or so stores and restaurants that
hadn't been renovated for at least half a century.

It was around midnight when we spotted a large motel in the
middle of town that resembled something built out of Lincoln Logs.
There were no lights on inside, only a long, buzzing neon sign out
front with the word *VACANCY* on it. Partially covered with snow,
the name Big Moose Inn above the entrance could barely be made
out in the moonlight. It had been constructed out of birch branches.
Just below the lettering hung a large set of moose antlers.

Approaching the porch, Maggie stared up at the branched
antlers. "What some animals will do to have a lodge named after
them, huh?" she said.

As we stepped onto the shoveled porch, a yellow overhead light
came on, illuminating our way. The front door swung open, and
a short, stooped woman in her sixties, dressed in a pink chenille

bathrobe and pink sponge curlers, stood in the doorway trying unsuccessfully to hold back a yawn.

"Excuse me. Come on in before you catch your death of cold," she said in a tired but hospitable tone.

Stepping inside the small, rustic lobby, I could immediately feel my ears beginning to burn from the warmth, but I didn't dare rub them. One case of frostbite in my life was enough. I set our bags down on a colorful American Indian area rug.

"Welcome to the Big Moose Inn. Gracious, I must look a fright. You'll have to forgive me," the pear-shaped woman said, yanking curlers out of her hair left and right and dumping them into the pockets of her robe. Unfortunately it did little to resolve the fright issue.

Lurking in the shadows behind our hostess, an enormous grizzly bear in attack mode stood motionless on its hind legs, wearing a snarling expression not unlike that of Elvis in his early years.

"Boy, he's certainly a big one," Maggie said.

The woman turned to acknowledge the bear. "Oh, yeah. Mean as the dickens, too. He's sort of our official greeter. We call 'im Old Yeller. Named 'im after the color of the drawers on the fella who shot 'im in self defense." Our hostess was a crack-up.

"Sorry about showing up this time of the night, but—" I began.

"That's quite all right. True enough, when we hit the bed tonight, we weren't expecting any guests. Then about ten minutes ago, I sat straight up out of a dead sleep, turned to my husband, and said, 'Herbert, we got visitors coming.' I just knew it. Right then I got a call telling me about the train mishap. I guess I'm just psychotic that way."

"You mean psychic?" Maggie asked.

"Well, yeah, that, too. I suspect others will be coming. Here, let me get those for you," she said as she reached for our luggage.

"Oh, that's okay; we can get these ourselves," Maggie said.

"Nonsense—part of the service." The woman deadlifted our bags, Maggie's two in one hand and the carpetbag in the other. Her upper body immediately tipped to the side that held Maggie's bags. She raised the carpetbag up in the air in her other hand as she waddled toward the registration desk with us following.

"But I'd swear this old carpetbag here is completely empty," she said.

"You'd be surprised," Maggie said.

"You'll have to forgive me. . . . I'm as slow as molasses in January these days, what with this dang arthritis and all. The name's Gwyneth, like that movie star gal. But I look more like a Gwen, don't I? Feel free to call me Gwynnie. That's what everybody calls me—Gwynnie." She set the bags down next to the registration counter and curled around behind it. She switched on a desk lamp, which wore a copper shade with holes poked through it to form a design around its perimeter. The lamp lit up a stuffed skunk with a nasty case of psoriasis sitting on the counter next to it.

"Aahh!" Maggie said, mildly startled.

"Don't get too close to ol' Stinky, there," Gwynnie warned with a chuckle. "He's been known to let loose on a few unsuspecting folks. I'll be with you in two shakes of a lamb's tail—just need a second to get organized here. Have a look around." Gwynnie flipped a nearby wall switch, lighting up an adjacent, step-down, A-frame lounge.

Maggie and I wandered off in that direction, stopping at the top of the three steps that led to the lounge. Above the entrance to the room was an enormous old saw with a wooden handle at each end. It had to be ten feet long. On the wall next to me hung a framed sepia photo of a group of heavily bearded, tough-as-nails loggers, some in derby hats, sitting on the trunk of a giant tree that they had obviously just felled. I was feeling farther away from home every second.

I looked down at the spacious lounge filled with old log-framed couches and chairs and a giant stone fireplace. A tall, fully decorated Christmas tree stood in the corner.

The high-gloss-varnished knotty pine walls of the lounge displayed the heads and hides of numerous animals, including deer, bear, badger, and raccoon. A huge moose head enjoyed the best view of the room from over the fireplace. Birds, rabbits, and squirrels, all frozen in various action poses, were scattered around the room on tables and shelves. Maggie gazed around at the display of animals, her eyes wide and her mouth sufficiently agape.

"What do you think they do for fun in this town?" I quietly asked Maggie.

"Well, if you're an animal, I'd say a lot of hiding. Listen, David, there's no sense in our getting two rooms, right? I mean, you're all right with that—getting one room?"

"Yeah, I guess."

"Don't look so worried—I'm not going to attack you or anything."

What did she mean by that? Did she mean that she wanted to attack me but would control herself because she knew I wasn't interested? Or was she saying, *Don't worry, I'm not the least bit attracted to you, you ugly, pathetic loser?*

"Okay, folks," Gwynnie said, standing behind the counter and sporting a pair of reading glasses. "I can check you in now."

We walked back over to the counter, and Maggie delicately

stroked the white streak on Stinky's back. "It seems very few of the animals around here actually move," Maggie noted.

"Well, the rats might take exception to that—seems they get around pretty good," Gwynnie said. After a moment of deadpan, she burst out with a single chortle. "Had you going, didn't I?"

"Yes, you did," Maggie said with an impatient grin. "Do you think we could get a room?"

"Well, I'm sure we can accommodate you."

"All we need is a place to sleep—nothing fancy," I said.

"Well, here at the Big Moose Inn," Gwynnie began with a new voice, a rehearsed voice full of additional enunciation and inflection, "we pride ourselves on the unique, individual motif presented in each room. Every room at the Big Moose Inn has been thematically furnished to relate to a specific animal indigenous to the surrounding area."

All I wanted was a bed and a soft pillow.

"Do you have a room with two queen-size beds?" Maggie asked.

Gwynnie turned around and peered over her glasses at the simple display board holding keys on hooks labeled to correspond to the various handwritten names of rooms. Leaving her pitchman voice behind, she said, "Rooms with two queens we have available right now . . . I can give you the Beaver Dam, the Deer Cove, the Rabbit Hutch, or the Rodent Den. Your choice." She lifted a registration book off the desk, spun it 180 degrees, and set it down in front of us on the counter.

I was so preoccupied with why anyone would actually choose to stay in the Rodent Den, much less offer such a room, that I didn't respond right away.

"We'll take the Deer Cove," Maggie said. "In memory of Bambi's mom and all."

"Excellent choice." Gwynnie lifted the keys off the hook by the key ring made from a three-inch, cross-cut section of a birch limb. She dangled the keys in front of us for a moment while looking us over. "You two are married, aren't you?"

Without missing a beat, Maggie leaned in toward her. "Why else would we want separate beds?" she said in a stage whisper.

"Just sign right here," Gwynnie said, handing over the keys to Maggie, while I scribbled *Mr. and Mrs. Connors* across the registration page. It felt like an act of betrayal on several levels. I handed over my credit card. "Up the stairs, down the hall on your left," she said.

I grabbed the bags. Maggie looked at the key. "But what's the room number?"

"Just match up the picture on the key to the picture on the door of the room," Gwynnie said.

Maggie handed me the key. "By the way," I asked Gwynnie, "what town is this, anyhow?"

"Honey, it's just a stop along the way. You two sleep well. Muffins, donuts, and coffee in the lounge bright and early. Oh, and by the way, there's a little Christmas shindig in the dining room tomorrow night that you folks won't want to miss. Good night." With that, Gwynnie slipped through the door behind the counter, closing it quietly behind her.

We climbed the creaky stairs to the second floor. Walking down the hallway, I looked at the tiny folk art vignette of a doe on the wooden key chain in my hand. We passed a door on our left displaying a crude illustration of a beaver building a dam. We kept walking.

"Gwynnie seemed nice enough," I said.

"Yeah, I'm sure she's a big hit with the local taxidermist."

To our left, as predicted, a door came into view, on which was illustrated a brown deer that matched the one on the wooden key ring.

I inserted the key, with a twist pushed open the door, and was greeted with a smell similar to that of old encyclopedia pages. Maggie and I stepped inside the room, and I turned on a light from a wall switch.

"Oh, my gosh," Maggie said, scanning the room. There were deer everywhere: deer paintings on the wall, a life-sized photo-mural of a white-tailed doe and her spotted fawn lying in the woods, little wooden carvings on tables, deer plastered across lampshades, deer images on area rugs, needlepoint bucks sewn onto throw pillows, woven deer on bedspreads, and a deer head mounted over each bed. It was a veritable deer purgatory.

"That's a lot of deer," I said.

Maggie couldn't take her eyes off the deer heads over the bed. "This is wrong. This is just so wrong."

I set Maggie's luggage down on the nearest bed and tossed the carpetbag onto a nearby chair. "And I suppose you think the bag led us to this room?" I asked.

"I do. Although I must say he has peculiar taste in decor." She took off her coat, draped it over the bedpost, and sat down on the edge of the mattress. "You still don't see it, do you?"

"Well, it's true that whole avalanche business was very strange but—"

"You keep saying how familiar all the objects are that come out of the bag, and they all seem to have a purpose. It's clear to me that they're leading you somewhere."

"Leading *me*? You mean leading *us*. The train ticket was for you." I took my jacket off.

"The bag only gave me that train ticket and promised me that job interview so that it could get you on that train. And he only got you on that train so he could bring you to this town. I wasn't sure about it at first, but now I am. This is your journey, David—not mine. I'm the one who's just along for the ride."

Her comment made me feel trapped, like I'd really been taken hostage by the bag. "Yeah, well, I don't like this whole thing one bit."

"You don't like it? *You* don't like it? I should be the one who's upset. In fact, I *am* upset." She stood up and began pacing alongside the bed. "This was supposed to be my vacation. This was supposed to be my big break in the publishing business. Am I in Florida? No. Am I going to New York? No. Instead I'm here in some little godforsaken place where dead animals go to be humiliated." She gazed up at the deer. "And it's all because of you and your stupid bag. So we aren't going to let that bag out of our sight, and we're going to figure out what the heck it wants from you and where it wants to take you—'cause the sooner you get there, the sooner I get my life back."

Maggie marched over to the bed, climbed onto the mattress, stepped directly up to the deer head, and stared into its beautiful, lifeless brown eyes.

"What are you doing?" I asked.

She took hold of the deer's sienna-colored neck and tried lifting it off the wall. "I can't possibly go to sleep with an animal carcass suspended over my head."

"Maggie, stop. I don't think old Gwynnie would appreciate your doing that."

When the deer wouldn't budge, Maggie became more determined, wrapping her arms around the deer's head, positioning her shoulder under the deer's chin, and thrusting upward with the grunt of an Olympic weight lifter.

"It's probably bolted down," I said. "You're going to pull half the wall down with it." I tried to envision feisty little Gwynnie's reaction to such a disaster, and it wasn't pretty.

Maggie refused to give up. "Will you give me a hand?"

"No. Come down before one of you gets hurt."

"Fine. I'll do it myself."

"I don't think so." I jumped onto the bed and approached Maggie, "Just let go of it." I grabbed either side of her waist and tried to pull her away.

"What are you doing?" she asked.

"Stopping you before you get us both in trouble." I circled my arms around her entire waist, securing a tighter hold on her. My body was pressed up against her back as I continued to try to separate her from the deer.

"Let go of me." She didn't let up and neither did I. She propped her foot up against the wall for leverage and began yanking away on Bambi's mom again.

She wouldn't let go, so I grabbed onto her left hand and one by one, pried her fingers off the head.

"Stop it," she said. I heard a snapping sound, at which point both Maggie and I flew back onto the bed, landing alongside each other.

Recovering, Maggie turned toward me on one elbow, a shock of hair cascading over her eyes. I brushed it aside to reveal a look not of displeasure but of bewilderment. She raised her other hand into view. It was still holding onto the deer's ear. Disgusted, she quickly dropped it onto the bed. "Yuck!"

We both looked up at the one-eared deer still hanging on the wall. "Look at what you've done to the poor thing," I said with a laugh.

"It's not funny. I've maimed it."

"You've turned it into Vincent van Doe." It was easily the corniest thing I'd ever said in my entire life, but oddly enough, it made her laugh. I wasn't sure if it was by accident or by design, but as she continued to laugh, she lifted her knee up onto my leg, sliding her thigh up against mine.

It took me by surprise—not the move she made, but the urge I had to kiss her. All those months deprived of physical intimacy had finally caught up with me.

Her laughter subsided into a smile. "This is no way for a married couple to act." She looked down at my mouth the way people in movies always do just before they kiss.

I rolled away from her and off the bed, landing on my feet. "I need to buy some clothes."

"What?"

"I don't have any clothes—I need to buy some."

"Right now?"

"No. In the morning." I looked up at the deer. "We should probably pick up some glue, too."

"Okay."

I thought I was handling the situation pretty smoothly until she sat up and said, "Are you all right?"

"Fine. I'm fine."

"Okay, well, I'm going to brush and get ready for bed." Maggie dumped the contents of her purse out onto the bed. Lipstick, spearmint gum, nail polish, a toothbrush, and an assortment of other stuff, including the sunglasses, spilled out. She picked up the toothbrush and then the sunglasses. "Maybe the sun will come out tomorrow." She smiled, grabbed her suitcase, walked into the bathroom, and closed the door behind her.

I picked the ear up off the bed and set it down on the night-stand. Walking over to the window and pushing the curtain aside, I couldn't believe I was seeing snow falling once again. Consciously I was thinking, *Has it really only been one day since I discovered the bag on that ledge?* Subconsciously I was wondering, *Why didn't I kiss her?* I pressed my nose against the cold glass, feeling as wind-blown as those snowflakes that danced outside in the darkness.

Ten minutes later Maggie emerged wearing a pair of pajama shorts and a blue T-shirt. She yawned, "I'm dead."

I ventured into the bathroom and found a fresh, wrapped, complimentary toothbrush sticking out of a plastic cup with a picture of a deer on it. It was just what I needed, and the bag hadn't given it to me. I brushed my teeth and returned to the cool, dark room to find Maggie asleep in her bed and pillowcases covering the two deer heads.

Stripping down to my underwear, I slipped into bed. I turned on my side, away from Maggie, one pillow under my head and a second one lying alongside my body to help me to remember what it felt like to fall asleep with my arm around Kathy, our bodies perfectly molded together. It seemed like a lifetime ago.

I didn't believe that the carpetbag had led me to that room, but if it *had*—for what purpose? Was it providing some cosmic traveling dating service with the intent to pair Maggie and me up, to help me get on with my life after Kathy? If that was the plan, the ratty old bag didn't know me very well. I pulled the pillow in closer to my body, not entirely ready to let go of my past.

ten

WHEN ANNETTE WAS A MOUSEKETEER

I woke to the sound of Maggie in the shower, singing "Somewhere over the Rainbow" in a key uniquely her own. Had a group of munchkins suddenly filed into the room to sing backup, I don't think I would have been terribly surprised. My waking hours were becoming more bizarre than my dreams at this point.

On the nightstand between our beds sat the box camera. Beside it lay the film cartridge that Maggie had evidently removed from the camera while I was still sleeping. If the camera had a purpose, I was sure it was only to provide Peter with a photo of himself to give to his girlfriend. In which case, yes, we needed to get the film developed. But Maggie's suggestion that there were undeveloped images on that film that could help us solve some personal mystery of mine seemed ludicrous.

When Maggie and a small weather system of steam emerged from the bathroom, I took her place in the now lukewarm shower. A few short minutes and a small battle with the toilet handle later, I stepped out of the bathroom, drying my hair with a towel.

Dressed in blue jeans and a yellow knit sweater, a dejected Maggie was sitting on the bed, hanging up the phone. "They were very understanding about our situation and asked me to keep them posted."

"Well, maybe they've managed to clear the tracks by now, and you can be on your way to your interview, and I can start heading home."

"You just don't get it, do you?"

Actually I was afraid that I *was* starting to get it — I just didn't want to admit it out loud to Maggie or myself.

We left the deerfest behind in search of the essentials: food, clothing, and news. Maggie took charge of the carpetbag, and we started down the stairs leading to the lobby.

"Why don't we grab some donuts here at the lodge," she said. "After that we can find a second wardrobe for you, then see if we can get the film developed somewhere."

"That's fine with me. I wouldn't count on this town having a one-hour photo, though."

We walked down to the lobby where a line of familiar faces waited to check in. "That's not a good sign," Maggie said.

Arlene Pickett was at the front of the line, signing the registration book. As we passed, Gwynnie looked up from behind the counter. "Good morning, Mr. and Mrs. Connors — sleep well?" Arlene turned around in time to give us a disapproving look.

"Yes, thank you," I said sheepishly.

As we stepped down the stairs to the lounge, I could see Peter standing alongside a buffet table displaying the breakfast spread. Directly across from him was Ethan, wearing Peter's army cap. Peter stood at attention with a donut in one hand, saluting the little boy with the other. Ethan imitated Peter's actions, jerking a stiff hand up against his forehead. "Good, that's good," I could hear Peter say.

Maggie also noticed Peter as he looked our way. "Great — now he's recruiting the next generation of killers. On second thought, why don't we go out for breakfast."

"Okay, but let's find out the train's status first." I walked up to Peter, while Maggie lagged behind. "Morning, Peter."

"Good morning to you," he replied.

"Hey, Ethan, how's it going?" I asked.

"Good."

"Is the plane still in one piece?"

"Yep. But my mom won't let me have it right now."

"Well, maybe when you get outside, she'll let you play with it." I turned to Peter. "What's the story with the train?"

"It seems we're stranded for at least another day."

"Oh, that's perfect," Maggie said. "Like I've got nothing better to do with my life."

"I wonder how far away the nearest bus station is," I said.

"It wouldn't do much good," Peter said. "I hear the roads are closed due to the snowfall."

"Great," Maggie said. "Well, if you'll excuse us, we're going to see if there's an actual restaurant in this town."

"Someone mentioned that Anderson's Diner down the road is a local favorite," Peter said.

"Sounds good to me," I said. "Would you like to join us?"

Peter looked at Maggie, who diverted her eyes toward the floor. "No. Thank you for offering, but I'm already on my third donut."

"All right, then we'll probably see you both later."

"Okay. Good-bye," Peter said.

As we turned to leave, Ethan called out, "Ma'am?" Maggie turned back around. Ethan stood at attention, clicked his heels together, and gave a convincing little salute. Maggie just looked at the boy for a moment, glanced over at Peter, then gave Ethan a return salute and turned for the door.

As we walked off, Maggie turned to me. "I can't believe you invited him to come with us."

"Why not?"

"First of all, because it's not like you at all, and secondly . . . you knew I wouldn't like it."

I took a moment to review my identity, and she was right. It wasn't like me at all to invite him along. Maybe I was still feeling like we owed it to him for the way Maggie treated him back on the train.

My stomach gurgled as we approached the glass double doors of the fifties-style diner. A few steps from the entrance, an elderly black man in a tattered red and green plaid coat and a soiled red hunting cap slowly waltzed in a circle in the snow. As he was muttering something to himself, presumably conversing with voices in his head, he looked our way. Maggie must have felt a certain apprehension about the man, because she handed the carpetbag over to me. "Here, maybe you should hold onto this."

I had a suspicion the man was going to ask for a handout, so I prepared myself by staring at my shoes.

"Spare change?" he asked in a quiet, throaty voice.

I never liked to accommodate beggars, but Kathy thrived on it. She'd hand out dollar bills like they were flyers for a bake sale. A soft touch if there ever was one — getting taken advantage of by every leech we ran into. She'd justify it by saying, "Well, Jesus said that he wouldn't recognize his followers if they didn't give to the poor." She was always quoting Jesus like he lived next door, like she had just spoken to him over the fence.

The problem for me was that half these bums weren't poverty stricken at all—just good actors.

"Sorry," I replied, without missing a stride.

Before we could enter the diner, a string bean of a guy in his twenties burst through the door, bellowing an obnoxious laugh. He wore a pea coat and a dull orange scarf with tassels at the ends. With a spring in his step, he swung his gangly arms about as if his body were being manipulated by a giant, invisible puppeteer. Following him out of the diner was a short guy, bowlegged as an English bulldog. He had protruding eyes and was dressed in a fleece-trimmed suede coat and stiff blue jeans.

When the duo noticed the panhandler, their laughter faded. The short guy threw back his shoulders and stepped right up to the black man's face.

"What's the deal, Rags?" he said. "I thought Ziggy and I made it clear we didn't want to see you around here."

I was reaching for the door of the diner when the old tramp squeezed the sleeve of my jacket with his soiled green gloves, forcing me to stop and look at his face. His skin was thick, covered with a scattering of white stubble. Phlegm-yellow eyes filled with desperation looked up at me from just beneath the bent-down brim of his hat.

"Sir, please," the old man said. "I'll pay you back."

With a goofy grin Ziggy said, "Yeah, man, he's just waiting on his Christmas bonus." The short friend responded with a machine-gun tatter of juvenile laughter.

Then the old man raised his hand and gave me what looked

like the Cub Scout salute. "I promise," he said, giving his pledge. This was an approach I hadn't seen before.

"Nice touch, Rags, but aren't you a little old to be a Boy Scout?" the short man said.

Either the old geezer was truly sincere or as good as De Niro.

"Look . . . I may have some change," I said, reaching into my pocket.

Maggie stopped me. "David, maybe he'd like that thing."

"What thing?" I asked her.

"You know . . . that thing in the bag."

Unfortunately I wasn't getting a sense of any *thing* being in the bag. Possibly Maggie was just hoping for something to materialize, but I didn't appreciate her putting me or the bag on the spot.

"Hey, chief," the little guy said to me, stepping between me and the vagrant, "this bum's been hanging around here for about a week now. We don't need some outsider encouraging the old fart."

I wasn't in the mood for a confrontation. "Maggie, he's right. This is really none of our business."

She looked at me like I'd just stuck carrots up my nostrils. Then she gently placed her hand on the old man's shoulder. "What's your name?"

"John. John Newton," he said, as if it were an admission of guilt. I felt sorry for the old man.

"It's okay," Maggie said to him. "We'll give you something."

No sooner had Maggie's words turned to wispy white steam than the carpetbag seemed to gain the slightest weight. I gave the bag a little jiggle, confirming that it was no longer empty.

I spread the top of the carpetbag open wide enough for only my eyes to see inside. I could make out an old baseball rolling along the bottom. I looked over at John, feeling certain this was not going to help his cause. "I'm afraid I don't have anything you can use," I said, and closed up the bag.

"See, old man, you're out of luck—so beat it," the tall marionette said.

"I'll take whatever you've got," John said. He looked as if he had faith that there was actually something of value in the bag, adding to my suspicion that he might be senile. All the more reason not to disappoint him.

Maggie leaned over to me, whispering, "Whatever it is, give it to him."

Against my better judgment, I split the top of the bag open again, reluctantly removed the ball, and placed it in his cupped, green-gloved hands.

"Thank you," he said, grinning like I'd just handed him a million bucks. Now I was sure he was crazy. At the same time, though, I had made him happy. And in the most basic of ways, it made me feel good.

Ziggy and his friend began to laugh.

"There you go, Rags," the short one said. "Just what you always wanted, a ratty old baseball."

"Hey, how 'bout a little catch, Butch?" Ziggy snatched the ball from John's grasp and tossed it over John's head to his friend. John stumbled forward toward Butch in an attempt to retrieve the ball, but Butch flung it just out of his reach, back to Ziggy.

"You're gonna have to do better than that, old man," Butch said.

"Come on, guys," I said. "Give him the ball back." But the two of them were having too much fun at John's expense to give up the game.

"Hey, guys, you must have something better to do with your time, right?" Maggie said.

"That depends. What do you got in mind, sweetheart?" Ziggy asked, reaching over and fondling Maggie's hair.

"A shower, now," she immediately replied, recoiling in disgust.

Bravery in the face of bullies had never been my strength, but I couldn't stand to watch another second of the humiliation. I handed the carpetbag to Maggie, and when Butch tossed the ball back toward Ziggy, I leaped in front of him and picked it out of midair.

"Hey! What do you think you're doing, man?" Butch said.

I immediately handed the baseball back to John.

"Game's over," Maggie said. "Now run along and find somebody your own IQ size to pick on. Maybe a stuffed moose."

"You better hope our paths don't cross again," Butch said.

"Good-bye, now," Maggie said with a sarcastic wave.

Ziggy and Butch slowly took off in the direction of the parking lot.

"You going to be all right?" Maggie asked John.

"Fine. Thank you."

I opened the door to the diner, and Maggie entered in front of me. I looked back at John through the door. He held the ball up and nodded to me with a smile.

"Welcome to Anderson's, folks," said a tall man with a gray crew cut standing behind the counter. "Just find yourselves a table anywhere, and a waitress will be right with you."

The place was jumping, full of faces that surely belonged to locals. With the smell of strong coffee and scrambled eggs in the air, Maggie and I walked down to a window booth located in the middle of the diner. The red vinyl squeaked as we sat down on the cushions across from each other. The gray Formica table displayed a boomerang pattern. "Do you believe those jerks?" Maggie said.

"Small town — nothing better to do, I guess."

"Maybe we should call the police. They did threaten us."

"They're just harmless punks."

Maggie turned her attention to the small metallic jukebox at the window end of the table. "This is pretty nifty. Haven't seen one of these in a while." She flipped the metal lever across the face of the machine, turning the individual pages that listed the record selections. She took off her coat and looked around the room. "This is like a fifties retro diner without the retro."

And it was. Scuffed up black-and-white checkered tiles covered the floor. Tears in the red vinyl booth upholstery had been repaired with duct tape, hand-painted in an attempt to match the color. An old, bottled-Coke vending machine, dented and rusted, hummed in the corner, a wall clock circled with pink neon hung over the cash register, and a colorful but worn jukebox at the end of the aisle played a scratchy-sounding copy of "Mr. Blue" by the Fleetwoods.

It was as if Mr. Anderson had not yet been informed that Annette was no longer a Mouseketeer, that Ike had left office, and that a quartet called the Beatles had arrived from Liverpool and taken the American music scene by storm. The only thing he seemed to get right was a faded poster of Elvis hanging on the wall with the words "Elvis Lives" plastered across it.

The whole scene was a few years before my time, but I could tell Maggie was renewing an old friendship with the era.

"It's not bad for a greasy spoon," Maggie said. Bacon sizzled and popped on the grill, out of sight behind the counter. "It kind of reminds me of a place I used to go when I was young. Tinsdale's Diner — back home. It was a diner that had lasted past its prime. Not many people would even go there, it was so outdated . . . but Roger and I did. Late at night we'd cruise over there in his old

Studebaker and sit in the same booth every time. And he'd always order the same thing—a chocolate shake and fries with a puddle of gravy on the side. And we'd talk and talk into the night until we lost track of time. Funny . . . we never seemed to run out of things to say. Nowadays I can't think of a darn thing really worth talking about."

A cute young waitress with a sparkling smile pranced up to us and set a couple glasses of water on the table. "How are you two today?"

"We're okay," I replied.

"Well, great. Wow, that's a really big purse," she said, eyeing the carpetbag beside Maggie.

"You should see the size of my hair brush."

The waitress giggled. "My name's Judy, and I'll be your waitress today." She slipped two menus out from underneath her armpit and handed one to each of us.

"So what do you recommend?" Maggie asked.

"It's all good, but, personally, for breakfast I prefer the waffles with strawberries and whipped cream."

"That sounds good to me," Maggie said.

"I think I need some time to look at the menu," I said.

"Okay, well, I'll give you a few minutes to decide."

As Judy was turning to go, Maggie spoke up. "Listen, we were wondering, do you know of a place in town that develops photo film?"

"I'm not sure, but I think the souvenir shop down the road can help you out—Taylor's Gift Shop. Look for the giant grizzly carved out of wood."

"Thanks."

"You're welcome. I'll be right back." She pranced off on the balls of her feet.

Maggie leaned over to the jukebox song selector again and began flipping through pages.

"It was a baseball," I said.

"What? Oh yeah."

"So—what good was it?"

"To you or to John?"

"Take your pick."

"Well, for whatever reason, it seemed to give pleasure to John. Just like the plane did for Ethan. But as far as what it did for you . . . I guess only you know that." She dug into her purse and came up with some change.

"But it's not leading me anywhere," I said.

"Maybe it is, and you just don't know it."

She dropped a quarter into the slot of the selector, pushed a couple buttons, and I heard the coin drop.

"Find one you like?" I asked.

She tilted her head toward the jukebox at the end of the aisle. The song, "Wouldn't It Be Nice" by the Beach Boys, began playing on the jukebox. She smiled my way, nodded, and then looked out the window. I wanted to ask her the significance of the song, but I was pretty sure I knew it. Besides, I didn't want to steal her away from the memory, so I looked down the menu and came to a decision on eggs and bacon.

Maggie and I tracked down a general store in town that carried a small variety of clothing. Sawdust covered the hardwood floors of the place, giving it an outdoorsy smell. I picked up a couple long-sleeved T-shirts, sweatpants, briefs, and socks. Maggie held up a pair of blue-gray corduroys, mentioning that she didn't think I'd look horrible in them, so I bought them, too. I also decided on a red knit cap.

We went back to the lodge so I could change into my new clothes, and when we saw that the fireplace was ablaze, we did what people always do around a fireplace in December. Maggie relaxed in a well-cushioned, log-framed chair, her feet up on the hearth as she read the book that was supposed to keep her company at the beach. I collapsed in a matching chair next to her and picked up a magazine from a well-worn selection of year-old sporting publications. We looked like we could have been on vacation. And I guess we were: a vacation from the ordinary.

I found myself rereading paragraphs in an article on the art of fly-fishing. Thoughts of John Newton kept interrupting my concentration, making me keenly aware that it wouldn't take but a few small changes in my life's circumstances for me to wind up in his shoes.

I considered calling Kathy, but I realized that I couldn't very well explain where I was or why, or how I got here or how or when I might be getting back home. Besides, those words still buzzed around in my head: *I was hoping that I'd miss you.* There was no reason to think anything had changed. Looking back at the magazine, I had a feeling there was no one out there missing John either. In that respect my feet had already slipped halfway inside his shoes, trying them on for size.

eleven

A Decent Proposal

The tinkling of a strand of bells sounded our entrance to the quaint little gift shop. There were several tourist types wandering around and a few more making purchases at the counter —the place was loaded with handcrafted items. We made our way into the center of the store.

While Maggie lifted a small cedar box off a shelf and sniffed the inside of it, a rack of generic scenery photo postcards caught my attention. I picked out one with a sunset and one with pine trees, and checked out the backs. There was no indication of what town we were in. "Greetings from Nowhere," I said to Maggie. "See, I told you this town doesn't exist." I was only half kidding.

"Smells pretty real to me," Maggie said, setting the box down on the shelf. She opened her purse and dipped her hand inside. "Well, let's see if we can get this puppy developed." She pulled the roll of film out of her bag.

I looked over at the middle-aged man behind the counter. He was placing a package of note cards and an unidentifiable carved animal in a bag for a little girl. In any other town he might look out of place wearing a coonskin cap on his head, but here he fit right in.

"He looks pretty busy. Maybe we should just forget about it," I said to Maggie.

"Are you kidding? I don't understand why you don't want to figure this thing out," she said.

"I'm beginning to think that maybe there's nothing to figure out," I suggested.

She ripped the carpetbag from my hand. "This bag is leading us somewhere," she said. "Don't you feel it? He wants us to develop this roll of film."

"Have you been talking to the bag behind my back?" I asked, taking it back. "Because, personally, I believe that if we do get that roll of film developed, we're only going to wind up with one photo of a soldier looking confused and unhappy because somebody just told him what a fool he was for serving his country."

"I didn't mean to hurt his feelings."

"I know you didn't."

"All I'm saying is that if anything unusual happens, we should follow through to see where it leads us. There *is* a destination for you in all this."

"And what if it turns out to be a place that I don't particularly want to go?"

Before she could answer, I began to hear a tinny melody emanating from behind a nearby tapestry-curtained doorway. It was the unmistakable sound of a music box. Maggie cocked her head in the direction of the classical piece.

"Do you hear that?" she asked.

"No, I don't hear a thing," I lied.

Maggie squished up her face, attempting to hear the tune more clearly. "What is that melody?"

"Brahms's 'Waltz in A-flat Major,'" I answered.

Maggie looked at me like she had just discovered the meaning of life. "How did you know that?" she asked.

"Why? Am I right?"

"I don't know, but this is just the kind of thing I'm talking about, David. Let's go." Maggie stashed the film back into her purse.

"Maggie, wait," I pleaded, but she had already half-disappeared beyond the curtain.

I followed her anxiously into a dark, narrow hallway. The walls wore a busy, burgundy design wallpaper that was curling up at the seams, and the smell of mildew and mothballs permeated the air. "This is crazy—you're going to get us in trouble," I said as the melody grew louder.

"Yeah, well, maybe Trouble is my middle name," she said, continuing slowly down the hall.

"What? What are you talking about—Trouble is your middle name? What a dumb thing to say. Nosy—if you even have a middle name—*Nosy* is your middle name." This just wasn't right. "I'm going back." I turned to go, but Maggie grabbed the back of my jacket.

"Where do you know this song from?" she whispered.

The melody attempted to transport me to a time and place in my distant past, and while the destination was fuzzy at best, the feelings it evoked were crystal clear. There was something both happy and sad about the tune that probably had nothing to do with the composer's intent. But I recognized it.

"I don't know where I know it from."

"Then let's find out." She gave my arm a short tug. We followed the song to a door that was open just a crack.

Maggie slowly eased the door open. In the dimly lit room, a well-preserved elderly woman in bifocals lay propped up with pillows on a brass bed. She was wearing a white lace dress that looked like it was from about 1920. A shaft of light, slipping past a window shade and filtering through curtain lace, lit up her long silver hair piled on top her head. She was too absorbed in her old movie magazine — it had a glamour shot of Bette Davis on the cover — to notice us. A porcelain, cherub-crowned music box continued to play on the antique nightstand at her side.

I took Maggie by the sleeve and tilted my head in the direction from which we had come, hoping she'd agree that we shouldn't disturb the lady. But instead, Maggie intentionally cleared her throat. "Ahem!"

Startled, the old lady looked up from her magazine. "Oh, my goodness," she said.

"Sorry. We were just shopping and got a little lost," I said. "Excuse us." I turned to leave.

"No, wait. Please come in," the lady said. She set her magazine down on the bed.

"That's okay. We don't want to intrude," I said.

"Intrude? Don't be silly. I've been expecting you, James." Maggie raised an eyebrow my way.

"No, you see, I'm not — " I began.

"James and I heard the lovely music from the gift shop," Maggie interrupted. Proceeding to shove me into the room, she spoke into my ear, "Just play along with whatever she says."

That was the last thing I wanted to do, but as we moved closer, I noticed a cameo brooch at the center of the collar on the lady's blouse. Its ivory-colored carving of a woman's face on the stone appeared similar to the one that I'd given the cop. It was intriguing enough to keep me in the room for at least a few moments longer.

"I've always been partial to Brahms's lullabies," the old woman said. She reached over and touched the blond head on the rotating cherub on top of the antique music box. The device had a white porcelain, cylindrical base, gilded along the edges and on the angel's wings. The more I looked at it, the more familiar it felt. "I especially enjoy his 'Waltz in A-flat Major,'" she added.

Maggie shot a look my way. "It's a beautiful music box," she said to the woman.

"Yes, it is lovely, isn't it." The old woman pushed a small lever on the box, ending the tune. "You must be James's mother," she added.

For the next several seconds, Maggie resembled those animals back at the lodge.

With a smile I whispered a reminder, "Just play along."

"Yes, I am," Maggie said through clenched teeth.

"Well, you look so young for your age," the old woman said, minimizing the sting.

"Why, thank you. My name's Maggie."

"Come closer, Maggie," the old woman requested, and Maggie obliged. "I'm Elizabeth—Elizabeth Whiting." She reached out and shook Maggie's hand. "But I'm sure James here has told you all about me. It's so wonderful to finally meet you. And it's so nice to see you again, James."

The weirdness of it all had rendered my voice useless. But after Maggie delivered an elbow to my gut, I cheerfully responded with, "It's nice to see you again, too."

Elizabeth took a long look at the carpetbag, which I had forgotten I was even holding. "Why, James," she said coquettishly, "you haven't brought me something, have you?"

I could feel the beads of moisture on my upper lip doubling in size. The charade had to end, so I replied nervously, "No.

Actually, no, I haven't." From behind me Maggie's heavy hand on my shoulder pushed me down into a chair next to the bed.

"James, this is no time for frivolity," Maggie said. "Of course he's brought you something, Elizabeth."

"Oh, wonderful," Elizabeth said. "I love surprises."

"Yeah, me too." I slowly opened the bag on my lap, but couldn't make out anything inside. I gave Maggie a subtle shake of my head.

"Sometimes my son has problems finding things," Maggie said. She boldly took the bag from me. I wondered if she sensed something I hadn't, or if she were just taking another chance like she had with John. Obviously she had a confidence in the bag that I was still lacking. Stretching it open, she looked inside, hesitated, and then vigorously shook it upside down over the bed right next to Elizabeth. Out fell a toy ring.

Its thin, gold-colored aluminum band was split in the middle so as to be adjustable. Shaped like a diamond, a big blue hunk of plastic served as its jewel. It was the type of toy that years ago a little girl might have delighted in finding as a prize in a box of Cracker Jack or from a gumball machine.

Elizabeth's slender, violet-veined fingers reached down and gently picked up the ring. I tried to read disappointment on her expressionless face as she held the ring up in front of her. It caught a thin beam of light from the window, which gave it the radiance of a diamond—or at least the sparkle of a cubic zirconia.

"Oh, my word . . . it's beautiful, just beautiful." Between John and Elizabeth, I'd never met two people who could be so easily pleased. "I must confess, James," she said, composing herself, "I'd been having second thoughts about us. Will you forgive me for questioning your love?"

I was hoping I had heard her wrong. "My what?"

"Your love, James, your love," Maggie repeated to keep me in the moment. I felt like we'd all been horribly miscast in a really awful Tennessee Williams play.

And just when I thought the needle on the weird meter couldn't cross any farther into the red zone, Elizabeth said, "It's the most attractive engagement ring I've ever seen." She handed the ring back to me, extended her trembling, liver-spotted hand, and said, "Would you do me the honor, sir? Spare not a moment more, but speak the words from your heart that will forever remain in my memory."

I wasn't exactly sure what she meant. But then Maggie leaned over to me and whispered, "I believe she wants you to propose."

"Excuse me for a second," I said to Elizabeth. I stood and backed up toward the doorway, feeling claustrophobic. Stalling, I bent down and untied my shoelace so that I could tie it again.

Maggie walked over and squatted down next to me. "What are you doing?"

"Well, I can tell you what I'm *not* doing," I whispered furiously. "I'm not proposing to Katharine Hepburn over there."

"I understand your resistance. . . . Really, I do. But I think you need to do this."

"Are you crazy? Did you doze off? This whole thing is absurd. It's a Cracker Jack ring—and a Cracker Jack old lady to match!"

"But I think you're supposed to go through with this," Maggie said.

"Well, then, you need to change your way of thinking, don't you? I can't do this. It doesn't feel real. It feels like . . ."

"A play?" Maggie suggested. My silence told her that she was right. "Then think of it as a play. Be brave. Step onto that stage."

I looped my shoelace.

"Hearts are bewildering things, aren't they?" Elizabeth said to no one in particular. "They can be soft, pliable, innocent, open wide to all the possibilities that love has to offer . . . or they can become hardened from experience. And the difference might be but a single beat."

I had no idea what this old woman was talking about, but something in the way she delivered those words with such sincerity and conviction made me feel less anxious.

I finished with my shoe and looked over at Maggie. "I don't have to actually consummate the relationship, do I?"

I walked over to the bedside. Elizabeth appeared remarkably peaceful. I looked at her face, really gazed at it long and hard—long enough that she should have felt uncomfortable and said something. But she didn't. I looked past her silver hair, past the lines running from her clouded eyes down her rose-powdered, sagging cheeks, past her splotchy, translucent skin. And I saw Elizabeth in her prime—her thick auburn hair piled on top of her head, her smooth, milky white skin, and her beautiful blue eyes, clear and filled with hope.

I got down on one knee, and with a sincerity that rose up in me from an unknown source, I took Elizabeth's soft, smooth hand and asked, "Will you, Elizabeth, marry me?"

The old woman replied, "Oh, yes, Mr. James Oswald Emerson, I will, I most definitely will."

I slipped the toy ring onto her finger. She arched her fingers back toward her face for a better look at the ring. She smiled, moved to tears. As peculiar as the moment was, it sent a rush of compassion through me—a feeling so foreign that I almost didn't know what it was. I stood up and took a step back toward the door.

"Well, we should probably get going," Maggie suggested, moving to my side.

"If you must. It was so nice meeting you, Maggie."

"The pleasure was all mine, Elizabeth." Maggie looked over at the music box.

"Please, take it with you," Elizabeth said.

"Excuse me?"

"The music box. I noticed you admiring it. I want you to have it."

"Oh, no, I couldn't."

Elizabeth leaned forward, picked up the music box, and offered it to Maggie. "It would only add to my happiness," she said with a smile.

Maggie carefully took the gadget. "Thank you."

The light sneaking through the window faded, leaving the elderly woman covered in shadows. She barely raised her hand to wave before leaning back against the pillows and closing her eyes.

We quietly slipped into the hallway and closed the door behind us.

"It was just a plastic Cracker Jack ring," I said again, still amazed, as we began walking down the hallway.

"To her it was a diamond." Maggie looked down at the music box, which she held gingerly. "I can't believe she gave this to me."

We pushed aside the curtain and found ourselves back in the gift store.

"You recognize this music box, don't you?" Maggie asked.

I had remembered it the moment we walked into Elizabeth's room. "Yeah."

"So who did it belong to?"

"I'm not sure. I only remember . . . I could never get it to work, but there was this girl . . ."

"Who?"

"A little girl . . . she was the only one who could get it to play."

"Who was she?"

"I think she—"

"You folks need any help?" the storeowner asked in a pleasant, singsong voice as he approached us.

"Oh, yes," Maggie said, "someone mentioned that you might be able to process a roll of film for us." She pulled the film out of her pocket and handed it to the man.

"Sure. Oh . . . black-and-white film. Not a lot of call for black-and-white these days. We could send it out today, and, depending on the weather, get it back to you by next Friday or Saturday."

"You see, the thing is"—Maggie shook her head—"we'd need to get it back today."

"I'm afraid that won't be possible. Sorry."

"Well, thanks anyway," I said, aware of Maggie's disappointment.

He handed the film to me and turned around to adjust a family of small ceramic geese on the shelf.

"I guess it wasn't meant to be," Maggie said, though I could tell that she wasn't convinced of it.

"That's all right," I said. "Like I said, even if there were any old images on here to begin with, they've probably faded by now anyway."

"There are clues on that film, David. You just don't want to believe it."

The storeowner turned back toward us.

"You folks from the train that made that unscheduled stop?" he asked.

"Yeah," I said.

"Thank God no one was seriously hurt. My name's Harvey."

"I'm David, and this is Maggie."

"Nice to meet you. Listen, I used to dabble a little in photography. Still got a darkroom in the basement. . . . Can't guarantee the results, but if you're desperate . . ."

"We'd be willing to pay extra for it," Maggie said, looking encouraged.

Harvey took the roll of film back from me. "I'll see what I can do."

"Thanks so much," I said.

While we were walking up to the counter, Maggie said, "It's a nice little shop you have here."

"Thanks. I've had it for some time now." As he made his way behind the sales counter, he gestured toward the music box that Maggie was holding. "That's not something we carry, is it?"

"No," Maggie replied.

"I didn't think so."

"Your mother was nice enough to give it to me."

"My mother?" he asked, puzzled, placing the roll of film in an envelope.

"Yes," Maggie said. "You see we heard the music and, well . . . Oh, I'm sorry. I just assumed the elderly lady in the back bedroom there was your mother."

Harvey leaned on the counter, looking perplexed. "My mom went on to be with the Lord about ten years back now. And what bedroom might you be talking about?"

"The one down the hallway?" Maggie said, a little less sure of herself.

Harvey looked over at me for some help. "I don't follow. What hallway?"

"The one over here." Maggie walked over to the tapestry curtain that led to the hallway. "The one right h—"

She pulled the curtain aside, revealing a closet filled with a variety of cardboard boxes and junk. My brain tipped over inside my head.

Maggie looked at me, stunned. She closed the curtain quickly. Then she waited a moment before drawing it open again, apparently hoping the hallway leading to Elizabeth might magically return. It didn't. Maggie frantically searched the closet for a false wall and when she didn't find it, began pacing back and forth, panicked, like a small dog lost in the middle of a busy intersection.

Several customers stopped their shopping to watch the crazy lady.

"Is she all right?" Harvey quietly asked me.

No. And neither was I, but it was my turn to be sane and keep it together. "She's been under a lot of stress lately. What with the train deal and all," I said so very articulately. "Maggie, we should go."

"But you saw her."

"Yes, of course, dear," I said, giving the owner a look of sympathy for poor, delusional Maggie. I leaned across the counter toward him. "When her medication wears off . . . well, we just never know what to expect. Come on, Mags." She slowly tore herself away from the curtain. "We'll check back with you later about the film, then," I said to Harvey.

"Fine. Or I'll give you a call when it's done. Are you staying at the lodge?"

"Yes. And thanks." I herded Maggie toward the door.

"But you saw her, David. Tell him you saw her. And you proposed to her."

"Of course I did, dear," I said, shooting a reassuring look to Harvey as I escorted Maggie out the door.

twelve

THE SILENCE
OF ANGELS

Lunchtime rolled around, and though I was anxious to try a different restaurant, Maggie suggested we go back to Anderson's diner. I didn't ask why, but I had a feeling it had more to do with the ambiance than the cuisine. We took the carpetbag with us, of course.

Entering the packed diner, Maggie and I were greeted by the voice of Buddy Holly singing "Peggy Sue." The same guy with the crew cut was standing behind the cashier's counter finishing up a transaction. I guessed he was probably the owner, Mr. Anderson. "It'll just be a few minutes, folks," he said.

While waiting by the entrance for a booth to open up, I noticed two fish mounted on the wall behind Mr. Anderson. One fish was a bluegill no bigger than the one Jeremy caught at Long Lake a couple years ago; the other, a three-foot-long northern pike, displayed rows of pointy teeth and a fierce under-bite that made it look as unfriendly as any fish I'd ever seen. Below them hung two framed black-and-white photos — one of Mickey Mantle in the middle of a wicked swing for the fences, and the other of Joe DiMaggio down on one knee in the on-deck circle. Autographs were scrawled across both photos.

After a short wait Maggie and I grabbed a window booth overlooking a snow-covered lawn. Outside our window, dressed in a red snowsuit and playing all by himself, Ethan attempted to fly his glider among the snow flurries.

We ordered a couple BLTs from Judy, but when they arrived, Maggie spent more time fiddling with the toothpicks that held her sandwich together than actually munching on it. I, too, was struggling to keep the phenomenon of Elizabeth at bay.

Maggie snapped a toothpick in two. She pulled the music box out of her purse and set it on the table in front of her. "This music box exists, correct?"

"Correct."

"Then it would stand to reason that Elizabeth existed, correct?"

I had abandoned the concept of reason two days ago when I found myself lying on my back in the snow, having survived the fall from my building. "You would think. At least now we know who the bag belongs to," I said.

"We do? Who?"

"J. O. E. . . . James Oswald Emerson."

"Oh, my gosh . . . yeah . . . right."

"Which, according to Elizabeth, is me."

"So you think maybe the ghost of this dead James guy is the one who's taking us on this trip?" Maggie asked.

"I don't believe in ghosts," I said.

"But magical carpetbags you're okay with."

"You think our friend Elizabeth, my fiancée, was a ghost?" I asked.

"No." Maggie ran her fingers across the cherub's golden wings. "I think maybe she was an angel."

"An angel?" I laughed. "Sorry, but I don't believe in angels either."

"Well, you'd better start believing in something pretty quick here — you're running out of options."

"Kathy was always trying to convince me that angels were real. She said we all have guardian angels flying around us all the time . . . following us everywhere. I once asked her why my mom's guardian angels weren't around when she lay in her bed dying."

"What did she say?"

"She said, 'They *were* there . . . holding her in their arms . . . whispering to her about the wonders of heaven.' What else could she say?"

Judy pranced up to our table. "Everything all right here?"

"Fine," Maggie replied.

Judy noticed the music box. "Oh, that's cool. What is it?"

"It's a music box," Maggie said. "It's beautiful, isn't it?"

"Yeah. I love music boxes. Where'd you get it?"

"An angel gave it to her," I said. "What do you think about that?"

Before she could answer, Maggie butted in. "You see, David, here, isn't a big believer in angels."

"Oh, that's too bad," Judy said. "But then again, if angels really do exist, the fact that *you* don't believe in them won't make them any less real, now, will it? Let me know if you need anything." She turned on her toes and took off down the aisle.

"I like that girl," Maggie said. She looked out the window at Ethan. The solitary boy was now standing motionless with his head raised skyward, eyes closed, catching snowflakes on his tongue. He looked cold and alone . . . and familiar.

"I never understood why kids do that," Maggie said to me. I considered sharing my mother's theory with her, but the poor girl had been confused enough for one day.

Just then I recognized a laugh coming from down the aisle. Over Maggie's shoulder I saw that Butch and Ziggy had entered the diner. Maggie turned to look. "Oh, great—just what we need."

The two characters walked down the aisle in our direction. It wasn't so much the demented glare that Butch gave me as he passed our table that made me uncomfortable, but the way his gaze locked on the carpetbag at Maggie's side before he took a seat with Ziggy at the counter. I moved the carpetbag to the space between me and the window, took hold of the key that dangled from the gray shoelace, inserted it into the brass lock, and turned it ninety degrees to lock it.

"You mentioned something back in the store about remembering the music box," Maggie said, ignoring them. "And something about a little girl."

"Yeah. There was a little girl I knew when I was a kid . . . blonde . . . long blonde ponytail." I dug my thumb and fingernail into the folds on the knot of the shoelace that was looped around the handle.

"What are you doing?"

I managed to untie the knot and take the shoelace with the key off the handle. "I thought this might be safer, that's all." In the past few days so many objects had come to feel familiar to me that I probably shouldn't have felt surprised to sense a connection with the shoelace and the key as I stared down at them in my palm. But I was surprised and confused as usual. I tucked them into my pocket.

"Who was she?"

"What?"

"The girl—who was she?"

"Oh. She lived in my neighborhood, I think. She had a music box like this one—same song, same little angel on top. The reason I remember it is because it would never work for me . . . but she'd just have to touch it, and it would start playing. It was like magic."

Maggie turned the switch on the box, but nothing happened. "Well, apparently you're not alone."

"Maybe it needs to be wound."

Maggie twisted a key in the back and tried the switch again. Nothing. "So what became of her—the little girl?" Maggie asked.

"I don't know. My family moved away. I never saw her again."

"Out!"

The restrained shout came from behind the counter. Mr. Anderson was addressing John Newton, who had just entered the diner. Anderson removed his tortoiseshell glasses and let them dangle from their lanyard around his neck. "I've told you before," he continued, lowering his voice and walking out from behind the counter to avoid any further distraction to the customers, "you can't just wander in here anytime you want."

The old man remained standing by the entrance, rubbing his glove-covered hands together as some of the customers took notice.

"Hey, look," Ziggy said, "it's Rags!" The two clowns swiveled around on their stools, anxious to witness the humiliation.

"You heard me," Mr. Anderson said to John. "This ain't no warmin' house. We do business in here. You'll have to leave."

Anderson approached John, but the old guy held his ground. In a soft but determined voice, he said, "I'd like something to eat."

"And I suppose you've panhandled enough money to actually pay for something?"

John clumsily dug into the pockets of his tattered plaid jacket. To the amusement of Ziggy and Butch, he proceeded to remove an empty beer can, a stained handkerchief, a wrapper of some sort, a book of matches, which fell to the floor, and some sticky gumlike substance.

It was difficult to watch, but Maggie and I couldn't look away.

Finally, John pulled the baseball I had given him out of his pocket. He fumbled it from his gloved hand, and it fell to the tile floor with a *thunk*, rolled a few feet away, and came to rest up against Judy's white sneakers as she waited on a nearby table.

"Hey, nice pitch there, Rags," Butch said, evoking spitting laughter from Ziggy.

Judy picked up the baseball.

"You can have the ball," John said quietly to the owner.

You could tell that Mr. Anderson felt sorry for John, but business was business. He shuffled himself back behind the counter. "Just show the man out, Judy," he said.

"But Mr. Anderson—" Judy said, looking at the ball.

"Please, just take care of it, Judy."

"But the ball has some writing on it." Judy held the ball up.

"What's it say?" Butch asked. "Will pitch for food?" Ziggy joined him in laughing at the old man.

"No," said Judy, "it says, *Babe Ruth*."

Ziggy and Butch stopped mid-laugh, leaped off their stools, and dashed over to Judy. Butch ripped the ball out of her hand to have a look at it.

"Let me see that," Mr. Anderson said, breaking through the small crowd and taking the ball from Butch. He set his glasses on the tip of his nose and held the ball up close to his face. "Where'd you get this?" he asked John in an accusatory tone.

"I took it from that man over there," John said sheepishly, pointing in my direction.

Mr. Anderson walked directly over to our booth and handed me the ball. "On behalf of our town, I apologize," he said. He looked down the aisle at John. "I knew he was a drunk and a bum, but I didn't know he was a thief as well. Now, get out of here!" he yelled at John.

"Wait," I said. "I *gave* him the ball."

"What?" Confused, Mr. Anderson scrunched up his eyebrows.

"I gave it to him."

"Is it authentic?" he asked.

I cradled the ball in my hand, placing my fingers across the red seams. They were no more faded than the last time, when, with a much smaller hand, I had held what I was sure was that same ball. I gazed at the signature that had been scrawled across the bridge of the creamy-gray cowhide with the same bold intensity as the legend had lived his life, and I remembered.

"It was my dad's. He told me that when he was a kid sitting in the center field bleachers at Comiskey Park one day, Babe Ruth sent a long screaming line drive in his direction. And as it sailed over the fence for a home run, a bunch of hands in front of my dad reached up to catch it, but the ball was hit so hard . . . it was too hot to handle. It ricocheted off all those hands, popped up in the air, and landed right in my father's lap."

I looked up at Mr. Anderson. "At least that's the way he used to tell me it happened. After the game my dad and granddad waited for the Yankees to come out of the locker room, and when they did, the Bambino signed it for him. And when I was just a kid my dad gave it to me. This is that ball." I looked over at Maggie.

"And you're telling me you just gave it away to that bum over there?" Anderson asked, obviously puzzled.

"And he just gave it to you," I said, handing the ball back to him. "I figure it should be worth at least a year's worth of lunches for Mr. John Newton." Mr. Anderson stared at the ball for a moment, trying to sort things out.

"Fine. There's a table over in the corner. He can—"

"No," I said. "John will be joining us for lunch today."

Mr. Anderson briefly examined the ball again. "Right." He looked down the aisle at John and waved him in our direction.

Judy slowly escorted John away from Ziggy and Butch toward our table. Maggie slid over in the booth. "Here, sit here." John sat down next to her, across from me.

Mr. Anderson retired behind the counter, still studying the baseball. Butch and Ziggy quietly walked back to their stools.

Judy set the book of matches in front of John. "I believe these are yours," she said as sweetly as if he were her favorite uncle.

"Thank you," he replied.

"Now what can I get you, Mr. Newton?" she asked.

"Soup? Do you have soup?"

"Vegetable, potato, or split pea? Personally, I recommend the vegetable."

"Okay, then. That will be good. Thanks."

Judy walked off.

John stared down at the book of matches for a second, then looked up at me with eyes full of gratitude. He removed the glove from his right hand, placed his fingers on the red matchbook, and methodically pushed it over in front of me. "Please, take these."

"Oh, that's okay. You can keep them. I don't smoke or anything so . . ."

"Please," John said.

Maggie nudged me under the table and nodded for me to take them.

She was right. Unconditional charity was something I never felt comfortable with myself. If John had a need to pay me back, even if it were in this smallest of ways, who was I to deny him? I picked up the matches and stashed them in my coat pocket. "Thanks."

The three of us didn't talk much. Maggie and I knew all we needed to know about John, and maybe he knew all he really needed to know about us. And though I was curious as to where he came from and how he found himself in this vagrant lifestyle, I respected his privacy. Maggie ordered cheesecake for dessert, and we shared it.

It was funny about the baseball—I tried to remember what had become of it. Had it disappeared into another dimension the way socks sometimes do, and now turned up here, in this time and place? I was very young when my dad gave me that ball—too young to appreciate what the gesture meant to my dad and what it should have meant to me. The bond my dad shared with his father certainly had to be stronger than the one I experienced with my dad. Depositing a forkful of cheesecake into my mouth, I wondered who was at fault. Did he let me down, or was it all my doing? Or did the departure of the woman in our life simply leave a void that neither of us knew how to fill?

Outside, Ethan tossed his plane up into the air again. His frustration was evident. His shoulders sloped forward, and his head hung down as he bent over to pick up the plane after one more unsuccessful flight.

"Ain't easy to fly without help," John said, looking out at Ethan.

"Excuse me for a minute." I slipped out of the booth and left the bright warmth of the diner to face the cold gray skies filled with flurries.

After a couple turns of the propeller, Ethan heaved the wooden plane up into the air. It flew only a few yards, landing nose-first in a pile of snow just in front of me.

I picked up the airplane and brushed off the snow. "Need some help?" Ethan nodded. I held onto the thin balsa body of the plane with one hand while winding up the propeller with the forefinger of the other.

"You see, the trick is to not wind it up too much or too little." The long, fat rubber band beneath the body of the plane began to double knot. "And then, once you've got it all wound up, you need to hold on tight to the propeller with your left hand like this, and don't let go until you actually throw the plane." I demonstrated a throwing motion without letting go of the plane.

"Are you ready, Ethan?"

"Yeah!"

"Okay." I carefully handed him the plane, making sure his fingers held the wound-up propeller in place. "Rear back, and give it your best throw."

Ethan lifted his left leg up, drove his little body forward, and let go with a terrific throw, sending the plane sailing toward the gray clouds, arching at a forty-five-degree angle. The boy squealed with delight and danced after it.

I looked up to the sky and watched the plane catch an updraft, bank, and begin to circle. As I spun around to follow its progress, I was quickly overcome with a nausea that caught me totally off guard. I watched the glider fly into the branches of a tree while the sky closed up for me like the end of a silent movie.

"David?"

In the void I could hear my name being called, but I couldn't answer.

Gradually a hole opened up in the blackness, and Maggie's anxious face appeared. "David, are you okay?"

"Fine, I'm fine," I reassured her, even though I still felt considerably spaced out. Mostly, I was surprised to find myself flat on my back in the snow. "We need to get the glider out of the tree," I said, sitting up.

"It's okay—it didn't fly into a tree," Maggie said.

"Sure it did. I saw it."

Ethan arrived and stood over me, holding the plane. "You okay, mister?"

"Yeah, I'm fine, Ethan."

He dropped the glider onto my lap. "Do it again?"

thirteen

BUTCH, CHASTITY,
AND THE
GUN-DENSE KID

The carpetbag swung at Maggie's side, keeping time with her strides. We had begun walking down the main drag toward the lodge, but then opted for a more scenic rural route down a dirt road that ran alongside a wall of pine trees.

"So what happened back there?" Maggie asked.

"Nothing. I just got a little dizzy, that's all."

"You remembered the plane, didn't you?" She was relentless.

I did have a wooden airplane like that . . . but then again, "Every kid had a wooden glider like that."

"I'll take that as a *yes*. We'll just add it to our ever-growing list . . . train ticket, wooden egg heart thing, box camera, music box, Cracker Jack ring, autographed baseball, and now—"

"Mary Poppins said she wants her bag back, man," a shrill voice called out from behind us. Turning around, we saw Ziggy and Butch hustling to catch up to us. I sensed that they weren't just being sociable. With a concerned half-smile, Maggie handed the bag off to me.

"Yeah, we couldn't help but notice how you never let it out of your sight," said Butch.

Looking around for any possible escape, I saw an old mill on our left and a red barn coming up on our right. No other human beings were in sight.

"Must be kind of valuable. What other treats you got packed away in there, chief?" Butch asked.

Maggie and I kept walking.

"Hey, we're talkin' to you, man," Ziggy said as the two of them overtook us and blocked our progress.

Maggie, ever the peacemaker, said, "Don't you boys have a banjo duet to play or something?"

"Well, there seems to be a smart aleck among us," Butch said.

"What is it, exactly, that you guys want?" I asked.

"You see, we couldn't help but notice how charitable you've been with the contents of your bag there," Butch said, "so we figured you might want to extend some of that generosity in our direction."

"Figured wrong," I said doing my best Eastwood, while hoping that the tremors running through my body would be interpreted as weather related. "Besides, the bag is empty."

"So, then, you wouldn't mind us taking a look," Ziggy said, reaching for the bag.

"He said *no*," Maggie said, grabbing hold of the bag and pulling it out of his reach.

A crazed look crossed Ziggy's face, and he lunged toward Maggie's midsection and lifted her up off the ground.

"What are you doing? Put me down!" she screamed as Ziggy cackled, threw her over his shoulder like a sack of potatoes, and strode off toward the barn. Arms and legs flailing, Maggie still wouldn't let go of the bag. Butch sprinted after them as Ziggy carried Maggie through a side door into the barn.

Though they seemed too goofy to proceed with anything all that sinister or deviant, I raced up to the barn and through the door in hopes of a quick, efficient rescue.

The barn smelled of damp hay and manure. Waiting for my eyes to adjust to the dim light, I could hear the whinnying of a couple horses. My pupils finally dilated enough to reveal Ziggy standing off to the side, his arms wrapped tightly around Maggie from behind, struggling to keep her from squirming out of his grip. A pen of sheep shuffled anxiously nearby. Butch ripped the carpetbag from Maggie's grasp.

"Let go of me, you idiot," Maggie shouted.

"But you're such a pretty girl," Ziggy said, as though he were speaking to a poodle.

"Save it for the sheep," Maggie said.

"Let go of her," I said in a calm voice that masked a growling rage inside me.

Ziggy looked over to Butch, who nodded.

"No problem, man." Ziggy released Maggie, who rushed to my side.

"What's the deal here, chief?" Butch asked, trying unsuccessfully to pry the bag open.

"What do you want with the bag, anyway?" I asked him again. "I told you it's empty."

"Then why would you be carrying it around?"

A legitimate question.

Upon closer inspection Butch noticed the keyhole on the bag. "A locked bag at that," he added. "Okay, let's have it—give me the key, chief."

"Don't do it," Maggie said.

"Give me the key," he repeated.

"Don't give him the key."

Ziggy removed a handgun from his jacket pocket and pointed it at Maggie's head.

"Give him the key, David," Maggie said.

As fast as I could manage, I dug my hand into my pants pocket, distinguished the brass key from the sundry coins, yanked it out, and tossed it over to Butch.

These guys were a whole lot more serious than I'd given them credit for, and it scared the snot out of me. I could see the same reaction on Maggie's face and knew I had to be strong. "You can put that thing away now, okay?" I said.

Ziggy lowered the gun. Butch took several steps over to a bale of hay, sat down, and worked the key into the lock. Less interested in the bag, Ziggy kept his distance, twirling his gun around his forefinger like the Sundance Kid.

My relationship with the bag had been an interesting one, to say the least, but I was more than willing to give it away if it meant we could walk out of that barn with the same amount of lead in our bodies as when we walked in. I motioned to Maggie to slip out the door, but she grabbed my arm, her eyes on Butch.

With a click of the lock, the top of the bag split open. Butch set the bag next to him on the bale and spread the top wide. He reached in and pulled out a thin book with a bright orange cover.

"What do ya got?" Ziggy asked, still spinning the gun.

Disappointed, Butch replied, "It's a book. It's a stupid kid's book." He flipped through the pages as if searching for hidden treasure.

"Really? Which one?" Ziggy asked.

"What does it matter? It's worthless." Butch chucked the book in my direction. It landed on a patch of straw at my feet.

I picked it up. "It's *Green Eggs and Ham*."

"You're kidding," Ziggy said, sliding the gun back into his jacket. "I used to love Dr. Seuss."

I opened the book to the first page. There, inside the cover, was a colorful sticker with the words, "THIS BOOK BELONGS TO." Just below them, the oversized letters, "D-A-V-Y," were handwritten with childlike precision in blue crayon. I remembered the day I wrote them. In that brief moment, as I read my name, a short breath of peace and satisfaction snuck into my chest. A moment later it escaped me.

"My mom used to read his books to me all the time, just before I'd go to bed," Ziggy added.

With Maggie looking over my shoulder at the page, I thought, *Mine, too.*

"*The Cat in the Hat* . . . now there's a classic," Ziggy said.

"Would you shut up!" Butch yelled. "Cover them again."

"But why?" asked Ziggy.

"Just do it."

Ziggy reluctantly pulled the gun out of his pocket and aimed it in our direction. Butch strolled up behind me and removed my wallet from my back pocket.

"I get it," I said. "The kind of panhandling that the old man does is wrong, but what you're doing here is okay?"

"Yeah, something like that." Butch took a few steps away from us and sat down on the barn floor against the hay bales. A stream of dusty blue light from a crack in the barn wall lit up his satisfied face as he pulled several bills out of my wallet.

"So what makes you think that we won't go to the police over this?" Maggie asked.

"Feel free, babe," Butch said. "Personally, I haven't seen many police around here. Besides, you two have a train to catch soon, don't you?"

Maggie turned away in disgust. Ziggy looked at me, smiled apologetically for his friend, and then lowered the gun.

Then I saw it. Beside Butch the bag slowly began to expand, as if it were taking a deep breath. The horses stirred. Just beyond Butch's shoulder, the smooth, angular head of a snake peeked over the top of the bag. Leisurely its body began to glide over the lip of the carpetbag. The snake's tan body was decorated with brown and black marks. It didn't take an Encyclopaedia Britannica for me to identify it as a cobra.

I gave Maggie's arm a gentle squeeze and nodded in the direction of the bag. She looked over at the cobra as it paused, slipping its tongue in and out of its closed mouth. "Oh, my gosh," she said softly.

It was at that point that I realized Ziggy saw it, too. Butch started counting the money and sorting through my credit cards as his friend cautiously called out in a low, warning voice. "Uh, Butch . . ."

"Hold on a second, you'll get your share," Butch said. The serpent gracefully stretched itself out onto the bale of hay just behind and to the side of Butch's head.

"Butch, don't move," Ziggy said.

"What's the problem, Zig?" Butch still didn't look up.

"Snake . . . to your left."

Butch slowly turned to look over his shoulder. There, at eye level, the cobra coiled and lifted its head up off the straw, fanning out its impressive hood, threatening to strike. Butch's face turned pale. As he averted his eyes from the snake, the wallet and bills dropped from his paralyzed hands.

"Shoot him," he said, like a novice ventriloquist.

About six steps away, Ziggy lifted the gun and pointed it shakily at the snake. He didn't shoot.

Butch's face began to glisten with sweat, as once again, he made his request through clenched teeth. "Shoot him now, you idiot."

But Ziggy still didn't shoot.

The snake raised its fanned-out head even higher into the air, swinging it around in a hideous dance. The hissing seemed to serve to both intimidate and humiliate its victim.

Ziggy grabbed the gun with both hands as if to take a more accurate aim. "Butch . . ." he began, his voice quavering, "when you said to bring the gun, I didn't think this kind of situation would come up, you see . . . so" — Ziggy began to lower the gun slowly — "I emptied the clip before we left. I didn't want anyone to get hurt."

I wasn't fond of Butch. Nothing he had said or done since I'd first run into the guy had endeared him to me in the least. But something was about to happen that wasn't going to be pretty or painless. Would this teach him some kind of lesson? Was that what the bag had in mind? Is that what Butch "needed" — a large venomous snake to take a hefty bite out of his face, possibly kill him? Or was it simply what Maggie and I needed? I considered all this in a millisecond.

Dropping the book, I took two steps to my left and pulled a pitchfork out of a stack of hay.

"David, what are you doing?" Maggie asked.

I circled around behind the snake as Butch remained frozen with fear. His eyes widened as the cobra opened its jaws and leaned its concave neck back, building momentum for the impending strike.

I planted my feet, choked up on the wooden handle of the pitchfork, and was about to take a waist-high, home-run swing in the direction of the cobra's upright body when the snake pitched forward and landed a bull's-eye strike right on Butch's schnozola.

The term *Aaaaaah!* does not even begin to describe the guttural, bloodcurdling cry that emerged from Butch's mouth at that moment. He leapt to his feet, grabbed the body of the cobra with both hands, and began struggling to yank it from his nose, all the while continuing to scream. We watched helplessly as Butch battled with the snake, grabbing its head and twisting and squeezing until, finally, the serpent chose to let go. Butch covered his face with his hands and, with blood streaming down between his fingers, ran out the barn door.

I jumped over the bale of hay and stabbed the cobra several times until its body lay lifeless on the floor. Alarmed, Maggie rushed to my side, clearly torn between curiosity and horror. I tossed the pitchfork aside.

Ziggy stuck his empty gun back into his jacket and walked over to Maggie and me, staring in the direction of Butch's exit. Then he looked down at the orange book on the floor of the barn. "Would you mind if I kept the book?" he asked.

I picked it up, flicked a couple stalks of hay off its cover, and handed it to him. He grinned a crooked smile. "He's not really such a bad guy . . . Butch, I mean." With that, Ziggy headed out, picking up the pace as he reached the door.

Maggie stepped over the hay bale, knelt down, and began collecting the scattered bills and placing them back into my wallet.

I stooped down next to the *S*-shaped snake and nudged it. Picking up the cobra by its midsection, I made a discovery: This snake was not what it appeared to be. In fact, it had a name. I remembered it: Sammy. The name I gave it.

I gently tossed the snake in Maggie's direction.

"Aaahh!" she screamed, falling onto her backside to avoid it. "What's the deal?" She heaved my wallet at me in retaliation.

Then she took a closer look at the snake, her face a grimace of disgust. Gingerly she picked it up with two fingers. She felt its pliable, synthetic texture and the visible seam that ran the length of its body. She scratched with her fingernail at the brown and black painted markings on its hood. The hood remained flattened in a striking pose. Maggie jiggled the snake. "It's rubber."

"Not too dangerous, but perfect for scaring little girls." I remembered doing just that.

fourteen

PHOTOGRAPHIC
MEMORY

D raped from the rafters of the lodge's spacious dining room and bar, strings of colorful Christmas lights illuminated the dark room, creating a festive and rustic holiday ambiance. At the far end was a small stage covered with an assortment of fur rugs reluctantly donated by the local wildlife. And what the five middle-aged musicians on stage lacked in professionalism, they made up for in passion, as the lead singer belted out a Joe Cocker-like version of "Mony, Mony."

The room was filled with people. Maggie and I sat at one of a dozen small, round tables that formed a semicircle around a hardwood dance floor. Bathed in a soft crimson floodlight, several couples of various ages danced, some with far too much reckless abandon for my taste.

The idea of a party appealed to me: festive surroundings, upbeat music, bodies in motion, small explosions of laughter detonating all over the place. I liked the rhythm of the thing. But the reality was that the buzz of conversation always left me feeling lonely. I admired how effortless small talk was for most people—pleasurable, even. I always found myself thinking, *If only I could possess their bodies, inhabit their minds*—just long enough for me to understand the mechanism, to see how the wheels turned and how the cogs meshed. Long enough to discover how it felt to be normal. But tonight it didn't matter to me if I felt alienated. I was there for one reason—to drink myself into oblivion in an effort to forget the magical mystery tour the day had turned out to be. I had just begun the process with a glass of Jack, neat.

Maggie leaned toward me and raised her voice above the band. "Moses."

"What?" I said.

"Moses—wasn't he the one who turned his staff into a snake?"

"Sounds like the right guy, yeah." Kathy would have known for sure. She always had her face buried in the Bible, quoting Scripture to me like she was reading the *Daily News*.

"We saw something biblical today," Maggie said. "Are you aware of that?"

I was. And it wasn't just today. I had always been dubious of all those miracles described in the Bible, mostly because the only miracles I'd seen in my life were the births of my children. But now I had less reason to doubt. The parting of the Red Sea, Christ healing the blind, multiplying those few fish into enough to feed thousands of people, raising the dead . . . Those things could have happened —and not by magic. Our carpetbag wasn't conjuring up magic, either, but something else—a power I'd given up belief in long ago. And I took little pleasure in having to compromise my beliefs.

The problem I had with Jesus was an entirely different issue. It was, specifically, the Scripture that the crazy guy with the rainbow wig always held up on his big sign at the televised football games: John 3:16.

I used to rationalize that I never answered any of Pastor Neal's altar calls to confess a belief and commitment to Christ because it was too easy. To simply invite Jesus into my heart and believe that he died on the cross to cover my sins—that was all I needed to do in order to be given salvation? But the truth was it was too hard. Too hard, not so much because I doubted the miracles or didn't agree with Christ's teaching—because I did. What made it impossible for me to accept Jesus as my savior was that I *knew* I didn't deserve that kind of charity. For God to receive me despite all my screw-ups—how could I possibly accept that kind of forgiveness? Kathy used to say to me, "That's exactly the point. It was an act of unconditional love."

"The fun and games are over." Maggie reached into her open purse on the table in front of her and pulled out some ChapStick.

"The bag's really starting to scare you, isn't it?" I asked.

"It's not just the bag that scares me." Maggie stared at me like she was trying to x-ray my brain. "Who exactly are you, David? Really."

"What are you talking about?" I took a drink.

"Who are you to wind up with a bag like that? It knows you. That bag knows your history—maybe even better than you do. How can that be?" Maggie drew the ChapStick across her lips.

"I don't know. Maybe you should ask the bag."

She made a face. "You need to—"

"Drink. I need to drink. Okay?" I drank.

"So that's it, huh. When the going gets tough, the tough get drunk?"

"Who ever said I was tough?"

"Certainly not Kathy. And maybe I'm being naïve here, but I think you could be. But not with alcohol on your breath."

I set the glass on the table and stared at her.

"Somebody wants you to remember. Somebody's trying to tell you something, and I think sooner or later you're going to have to listen."

It was true that I still wasn't ready to listen. I didn't understand my fears exactly. I only knew that something was closing in, trying to clarify itself to me, making me begin to feel what I didn't want to feel.

I noticed the pink sunglasses sticking halfway out of Maggie's purse. I picked them up and slid them on. They fit tightly against my temples. "What do you think — good look for me?"

Maggie stuffed the lip balm back in her purse. "Things aren't the same anymore, David."

She was right. Things had changed since breakfast. The carpetbag had lost its innocence. I thought I was beginning to understand the nature of the bag, but now that it could conjure up a child's book in one breath and a venomous snake with the next, it was as much a stranger as the day I'd found it. No longer that timid child that amused us with its gifts, the carpetbag had matured to display a power that neither Maggie nor I was ready to deal with. Suddenly we were the sorcerer's apprentices. It was that awareness that led to our unspoken decision to leave it back in our room that night.

As much as I wanted to leave the carpetbag business behind, I couldn't help but focus on that Dr. Seuss book and remember how my mom sat up at bedtime reading with me. "I do not like them in a house," she'd read out loud, and I'd finish the rhyme, "I do not like them with a mouse." Just thinking about it made me feel like I was five years old again. More than that, it made me want to *be* five years old again — to simplify my life, to be safe in the company of someone who loved me. It also made me want to sit with Kelly before her bedtime and read her a book. I wondered if I'd get that chance again.

Maggie looked over at me. "You look foolish in those; you know that, right?"

I didn't care.

"Here, let me have them." As she reached for the sunglasses, her elbow connected with my glass, toppling it over onto the table. "Oops, I'm sorry," she said.

I didn't grab the glass and set it upright right away, but instead watched the amber liquid flow out onto the table to be absorbed by the tablecloth. I could tell by Maggie's expression that she was pleased by my lack of reaction, though I don't believe she had knocked over my drink on purpose.

"Nice sunglasses," Peter said, walking up behind Maggie's chair. He was still dressed in his army uniform, holding his cap in his hand.

Maggie stubbornly kept quiet, turning only halfway around to acknowledge him.

"How are you doing, Peter?" I said, raising my voice above the faux Joe Cocker's and removing the sunglasses.

"Anxious to get home, but otherwise, I'm doing okay."

Peter leaned over to Maggie. "Listen, I just wanted to say that I'm sorry about what happened on the train. I didn't mean to upset you."

My fear was that Maggie might defiantly stick her Make Love Not War sign in his face again, but instead she replied, "It wasn't your fault. I was just having a very complicated day."

"I was wondering if you might allow me to try and make it up to you," Peter suggested.

"That's really not necessary. But what'd you have in mind?"

"Well, would you care to dance? I'm no Fred Astaire, but—"

"That's very sweet of you," Maggie replied, "but the last time I danced to this kind of music, I think I was doing the boogaloo."

"That's okay. It doesn't matter how you dance," Peter assured her.

"You say that now, but it could get pretty ugly out there. Besides, you don't want to dance with an old lady like me."

"I'd consider it an honor," Peter said with sincerity.

Maggie looked over at me for help. "You can't refuse an honor," I said.

Peter escorted Maggie to the dance floor where they joined several couples of various ages strutting their stuff. The moment they began to dance, the drummer gave a final crash of the cymbal, ending the song to scattered applause.

The lead singer jammed the microphone into the floor stand and announced, "Thank you, thank you. We're gonna take a little break, but we'll be back in about ten minutes with more groovy tunes."

Maggie turned to walk back to our table. Then, over the speakers, Bing Crosby began singing "I'll Be Home for Christmas."

Peter must have called out to Maggie, because she turned back to face him. He extended his hand toward her as an invitation to a slow dance while the rest of the couples dispersed back to their tables.

Saturated in red light, Peter and Maggie began to slowly twirl around the dance floor.

I took out my blue ballpoint from my back pocket and began

mindlessly doodling on my paper napkin. The sketch became a pair of eyes, then . . . a woman's eyes. Light irises, long eyelashes, sleepy eyelids that framed beautiful, symmetrical eyes . . . and then I recognized them. They were Kathy's. I stopped midstroke, not sure whether I wanted to continue.

A hand on my shoulder made me turn around. There was Harvey from the gift store, holding a small manila envelope. "Hello," he said.

"Oh, hi," I said, surprised to see him.

"I was hoping to catch you here." He handed the envelope over to me. "Here are the photographs."

"Already?" I answered, but I was really thinking, *Photographs?* As in more than one? Maggie's suspicion was right. There *were* other images on that film.

"Yeah, I hope they're satisfactory. Like I said, I'm out of practice, so they aren't the greatest."

"Oh, I'm sure they're fine, but I could have picked them up at the store."

"Well, it sounded like they might be important. . . ."

Although I was anxious to have a look, I wasn't ready to share the experience with Harvey.

"Well, thanks very much," I said.

"How's your wife doing?" he asked.

"My wife?" It took me a moment to remember the weirdness in the gift store. "Oh, oh . . . she's doing much better, thanks."

"Good."

I was sure old Harvey was looking for something in return for his services. "So, uh, what do I owe you?" I asked, pulling out my wallet, fully expecting to be soaked.

"Nothing. It was my pleasure." He smiled.

Okay, now I felt bad. "No, I insist. I owe it to you."

Harvey raised his hand in resistance. "It was fun for me. Besides, we don't tend to keep score much around here. Tell you what — just do something nice for the next guy you run into, and we'll be even. Have a merry Christmas, David," he said, shaking my hand.

"Merry Christmas to you, too, Harvey. And thanks again." As I watched him weave his way between the tables on his way out, my heart sank a bit for having misjudged him.

I opened the envelope like I was about to announce an Oscar winner and removed a stack of three-by-five, black-and-white photos. On top was a picture of a large oak tree in a meadow. Looking closer, I noticed a tree house held within its branches. It looked familiar.

I slid the photo to the side to reveal the next one. Stunned, I stared at the blonde-haired figure, running away from the camera. Now it was clearly a little girl. At first I thought, *This is the dream I had on the train.* But a rush of emotions demanded something more, as real events, buried in my memory for a lifetime, suddenly surfaced.

I flipped to the next photo in the stack. The girl had a face, a cute smiling face, and something more. She was wearing a pair of cat's eye sunglasses. I picked up the pink sunglasses off the table and examined them, compared them to those in the photo. The two pairs were identical. They'd belonged to her. What was her name? I couldn't remember. Standing in the shade of the tree, the little girl was wearing Bermuda shorts and holding a Raggedy Ann doll under her arm.

The girl stared back at me, inviting me to revisit the time and the place, the smell of freshly cut grass, the summer sun on my skin, the breeze blowing over an open field, the sound of the little girl's laughter, and the melody of the music box that belonged to her.

As I sorted through the photos, the images lifted off the emulsion, compelled into animation by the memories: a blurry image of a dog running through the long grass, the girl climbing up a handmade wooden ladder on a tree trunk leading to the tree house, the long branches of an oak tree bending in the wind, and the girl rushing toward the camera with puckered lips. I remembered . . . she was always trying to kiss me, and I was always dodging her advances, fearing that I'd catch the dreaded cooties if she ever succeeded. I made sure I remained germ-free.

I shuffled to the last photo, the one I had taken of Peter on the train. I looked over toward the dance floor and saw Maggie settle her head on Peter's shoulder. The song ended, and I watched Peter place a polite kiss on Maggie's cheek.

There was something unexplainably private about the memories that I held in my hands, too personal to share with Maggie. Besides, showing her the photos would only bolster her enthusiasm for solving this mystery that I was content to leave unsolved. I stashed all but the photo of Peter in my pocket.

Maggie and Peter strolled up to the table. "Thank you," Maggie said to Peter as she sat back down in her chair. "Would you like to join us?"

"No, I've got to get back."

"Well, thanks for the dance," Maggie said with a smile. "It was nice."

"Thank *you* for the dance. Sometimes it's hard for people to take a chance like that—especially when they're fearful or just uncomfortable with the situation. But I want you to know I would have understood if you'd turned me down because you felt too awkward about dancing. Good-bye, Margaret."

"Good-bye," Maggie said.

Peter turned and walked back across the dance floor. Maggie watched him go.

"Peter's not such a bad guy after all," I said. "A little peculiar there at the end, but—"

"Did you hear that? He called me Margaret."

"Yeah. I guess it goes hand in hand with all that military politeness—that 'yes, ma'am, no ma'am' stuff. So has he contacted Laura to let her know he'll be late?"

Maggie took a drink from her glass as she continued to stare off in Peter's direction. "I don't know. I didn't ask. Did I see you talking to the guy from the gift shop?"

"Harvey. Yeah, he brought over the photos."

Maggie turned back toward me. "So? Don't keep me in the dark—what was on them?"

"Oh, nothing, really. Just blurry black-and-white splotches."

I could tell that Maggie was disappointed.

"Really? I was so sure there was a connection," she said.

"The only photo that turned out was this one I took of Peter." I picked the photo up off the table. "Oh, shoot—I meant to give it to him."

"I'll give it to him," she said. I handed the photo to Maggie. As she stared at it, a look of horror came over her face. She dropped the photo like it was on fire.

"What's the matter?"

She seemingly couldn't speak. She just kept staring at the photo lying on the table.

"What is it? What's wrong?"

"Where—where did you get this?" she asked.

"What do you mean? I told you—Harvey just brought it over."

"No, I mean *this* photo," she said in a panic. "Where did it come from?"

"I shot it on the train. You were there. Don't you remember? What's the problem?"

With a trembling hand, she slowly picked up the photograph and reexamined it. "This is *Roger*," she said. "This is—"

"What are you talking about?" I began to think that she was playing games with my mind. Or losing hers.

"This is Roger. *My* Roger," she said in a whisper, tears welling up.

"Look, I don't know what you're talking about, Maggie." I took the photo from her and looked at it again. "This is the soldier that we met on the train. This is Peter, the guy that you were just dancing with."

"Oh, my gosh," Maggie said, quickly turning around and scanning the crowded room. She rose to her feet for a better vantage.

Across the room I saw Peter walking away from us, toward the exit. I stood up next to Maggie, and above the buzz of chatter and the voice of Burl Ives wishing us "A Holly Jolly Christmas," I shouted out, "Peter!"

Peter stopped and slowly turned around. But it wasn't Peter. I hadn't seen this soldier's face before, but he wore those heavy black glasses and had wavy brown hair, exactly the way Maggie had described Roger.

He gave Maggie a smile, placed his cap on his head, and continued on his way through the door. Maggie muffled a cry with her hand and started after him. I chased her as she juked her way between tables and past waiters in a halfback run.

We dashed through the door and into the lobby just in time to see Roger walk out the front door of the lodge. Maggie ran outside to catch up to him. I stopped by a large front window and gazed out at Maggie standing alone in the snow, frantically looking in all directions. I walked out onto the porch, down the walk, and up to her, at a loss for words. She was shaking like crazy.

"You saw him, right?" Maggie asked, desperately checking her sanity. I nodded. She spotted something lying atop the snow. She bent down and picked up a sprig of mistletoe.

fifteen

KING OF THE PHOLEAZIATS

If the disappearance of Elizabeth had shaken loose Maggie's marbles, the transformation of Peter into Roger had sent them spilling out onto the floor, rolling out the door, and down the street. As much as I wanted to help gather them back to their proper home, I wasn't so sure I was the right man for the job. My own marbles were disappearing at an alarming rate.

"Forget about it?" Maggie shouted, looking back at me with eyes blazing as she stormed into our deer-filled room. "Maybe this kind of thing is commonplace in your life, but I don't tend to get a lot of visits from deceased boyfriends." I closed the door behind us before she could slam it. "Why did he come back?" she wailed.

"What does it matter?"

"What do you mean, 'what does it matter?' Are you crazy? Don't you get it? Roger was Peter all along—all along."

"Yeah, I got that part. And, yeah, it's very weird. What isn't these days? But aside from the supernatural aspect of it, why should you care? This is the guy who was old news, right? He existed in a whole different life for you — isn't that what you said?"

"Yes, well, he suddenly showed up in the here and now, and I want to know why." Maggie stroked the mistletoe like she was hoping to coax some answers out of it.

"I don't think he suddenly showed up at all," I said. "I think he's been with you all along. It just took the bag to materialize him."

"What are you talking about?"

"Back in your apartment that first night . . . he was sitting next to you when you were telling me about the mistletoe. And he was there in your voice when we first met Peter on the train. And in the diner when you picked out the song on the jukebox, he was all over your face."

"What do you want me to say? You want me to admit that after all these years, I still have feelings for him? Is that what you need to hear?"

"I don't need to hear anything."

"Fine! I admit it! Sometimes he crosses my mind. And yes — after Roger, nobody could ever measure up. That's just a fact. But it's no reason for his spirit to suddenly crawl out of the grave to stop by and say hello. It's not fair. All these feelings that I've managed to bury along with him . . ."

"They hurt all over again?"

"*Yes!* Are you happy now?" she hissed. "He left this gaping hole in my heart that I've always known could never be filled."

"You don't really believe that," I said. "If you did, you wouldn't have been sitting in that bar when I met you, tearing that little umbrella apart and staring at the door."

"That wasn't me. That was an imposter. Oh, I have my moments when I fool myself pretty well . . . believe that there could be someone out there, someone who could step into Roger's shoes. But the truth always manages to come back around to bite me."

"And the truth is that nobody replaces the perfection that was Roger?" I asked.

"Yes. And maybe you can't relate to this concept, but I loved him."

"And you lost him. Get over it. This wasn't the real Roger tonight—it was just some ghost who showed up with a bunch of fungus." I grabbed the mistletoe from her hand.

"Give me that," Maggie said, snatching back the sprig.

"Who knows—maybe Roger was the imposter."

"Shut up."

"Maggie, you knew him for less than a year. You were only eighteen. Given time, who's to say he wouldn't have just turned out to be another one of us pholeaziats?"

Maggie hauled off and slapped me across my face. Then she cupped her hand over her gasping mouth as her eyes softened. She slowly backed over to the bed and sat down.

Maybe I deserved the slap, but I wasn't about to take back those words. She needed to hear them.

Maggie fell back across bed, arms stretched out to the side, hopelessly crucified. "The photo you took of Peter . . ."

"It wasn't a gift for him. It was for you."

"Yeah, well, I don't need gifts like that. Reminders of how I—"

"What? How you what?"

Maggie didn't answer, but instead curled up on her side.

I gazed over at the carpetbag resting on the other bed, looking innocent of all that had transpired. I walked over and sat down beside it. "You let one event cripple you for your entire life. Why would you do that—never allow yourself to move on? Maybe that's what this whole scavenger hunt has been about."

"What?"

"Starting over, starting fresh—Roger coming back for one final dance. Roger finally getting his chance to say good-bye."

"Roger? What about me?" Maggie asked, sitting up, resurrected. "*I* didn't get a chance to say good-bye. I didn't even know it was him until it was too late."

"Maybe this is not about you. Could be the world doesn't revolve around Maggie," I suggested. "Who knows? Maybe the closure is his."

"The man is dead—how much more closure does he need?"

She had a point. "So what's your explanation?"

"I have no idea. All I know is that a few minutes ago God showed me just enough of Roger to make my heart flare up with excitement, only to have the flames doused a moment later." Maggie stood up and began pacing.

I could see she needed someone to blame. "So it's God's fault?"

"I don't know . . . maybe. Maybe it's all God's fault."

"I don't think so. I don't think you're angry at God at all," I said.

"I am. And I'm not all that thrilled with you right now either."

"No, sorry—it's not me. You can slap me all you want, but I'm not the one you're ticked off at."

"Right now I hate your guts."

"No, I don't think you do," I casually offered up.

"You *are* a pholeaziat. You are the king of the pholeaziats!"

"So I guess I'm not like Roger."

"Nothing like Roger."

"So I don't suppose you'd tell him he was a pholeaziat."

"No, I wouldn't. Because he wasn't."

"So if I were Roger, what would you tell me then?" I stood up, walked around the bed and began advancing toward her, hoping I was leading her in the right direction.

"I don't know." She backed away. "Leave me alone."

"Come on, tell me — I want to know."

"Who are you now — Freud?" She kept backing away.

"No, I'm Roger. Come on, what would you tell me?"

"Fine. I'd tell you that I miss you . . . and that I love you."

"And what?"

"And that I want it back — what we had — I want to feel that again."

"What else, Maggie? What else?"

"I'd tell you that I wish you'd never gone off to that war — that stupid, stupid war!"

"Yeah, well, I had to go."

"No, you didn't! You could have gotten out of it."

"Not a chance."

"You could have stayed at home with me."

"How could I have done that?"

"I don't know! You could have found a way."

"I couldn't."

Maggie stared into my eyes   Roger's eyes. "Yes, you could. You needed to stay with me. You needed to stay here where it was safe."

"They *made* me fight — "

"No, no."

"They made me go to Vietnam."

"But why couldn't you have died there!" Maggie screamed, pounding on my chest with her fists. I wrapped my arms around her, pulled her close, and she buried her face in my shirt. "Why did you come back? I *hate* you for that."

I was totally confused. "I thought you said Roger died in Vietnam."

"No. He came back home . . . shot up in combat. Scared, crippled . . . messed up in the head. He was so bitter, so depressed. I couldn't do it, David. I couldn't be there for him. As hard as I looked inside that mangled body, I couldn't find the boy that I used to know."

I held her closer.

"He said he didn't need me, didn't want anything to do with me. Not my love, not my pity. And he was right . . . pity was the only thing I had left for him. So I let him go . . . and then he shot himself."

"Oh, my."

I eased her down onto the bed, never letting go. I gently stroked her hair and rubbed her back. We didn't say a word. It was a sanctuary of silence—not just from the moment, but also from the madness of the past few days.

Finally Maggie lifted her head up off my shoulder. She pulled her hair, damp from her tears, away from her cheek and looked into my eyes . . . then at my mouth. She leaned forward, and we kissed . . . a small, gentle, instinctive kiss of gratitude. She looked up at me again, and followed up the show of affection with a longer, deeper, more passionate kiss, one that not only crossed but leapt way beyond the line of gratitude. I hadn't been kissed in months, and it felt spectacular.

But bumper cars were sliding around inside my brain. There were two roads that I could choose to travel at that instant. And while still locked in a deep, full kiss, I made my choice. The decision wasn't reached out of a moral obligation to Kathy, because, after all, I was pretty sure she couldn't have cared less where my bumper car took me at that moment.

And it wasn't that I hadn't found Maggie attractive. I had. And I did—especially at that moment. But I slowly broke away from her simply because she wasn't Kathy, and I wasn't Roger. And no matter how much pretending either of us might have done that night, we could never make that transformation—not in our minds, and especially not in our hearts.

The spray of hot water felt relaxing on the back of my neck as I watched the steam spill over the top of the shower stall. I'd always found the shower to be the ideal place to organize my thoughts. In fact, I usually became Einstein when I stepped into the shower. Closing my eyes, all I could think about was how good it had felt to hold Maggie in my arms a half hour earlier, to exchange those kisses . . . and how I had wished it had been Kathy who needed me like that. I wondered if she or the kids would ever really need me again for anything other than child support.

As the shower began to cool, I blindly reached down and twisted the hot water knob up a tad. The drain was sluggish; I could feel water rising around my ankles. The falling water sounded like gentle rain—a soothing, welcoming sound. The heat in the stall was making me drowsy, but I wasn't quite ready to leave its comfort. With my eyelids shut I could see *rain falling in the dark . . . on a warm, summer night.*

A little boy wearing a hooded slicker and holding a shovel ran through a field of long grass. A breath of apprehension filled my chest. *Black rubber galoshes splashed in a muddy puddle.* It wasn't just that the images felt so real—they were accompanied by a growing sadness. I opened my eyes and blinked, hoping to send it away.

I faced the showerhead straight on, closing my eyes tightly and letting the water spray directly onto my forehead, a sort of therapy, a distraction from the pictures in my head. I took a deep breath and began to relax again. Turning back around, I allowed the water to bombard the top of my head and stream down the front of my face. But the feelings and images quickly returned . . . stronger and more concrete than before.

Running in the rain, the boy stopped beside a tree. It was almost like watching a movie. Was it something I'd seen on TV that had crept into my subconscious and was now seeping back out?

The head of the shovel sliced into the rain-soaked ground, lightning flashed, a crash of thunder—and my eyes jolted open. The bathroom was blindingly bright for a second, as if lightning had actually struck the shower. The images were gone, but the feelings of fear and melancholy remained.

I finished my shower, dressed in a pair of sweatpants and a long-sleeved T-shirt, and walked into our room. I was carrying my jeans, and as I dumped them on a chair, I noticed the frayed end of the shoelace sticking out of the front pocket. I took it out and wrapped it around my fingers.

Maggie had fallen asleep in her bed with the TV on. Wearing a faded blue T-shirt and checkered boxer shorts, she was curled up in the fetal position. The sunglasses lay by her side. I picked them up and set them on the nightstand between our beds, then pulled at the corner of a bunched-up blanket and covered her up.

I sat down next to the carpetbag on my bed. The key was still inserted in the keyhole. I pulled it out, strung it on the shoelace, and tied the shoelace around the handle the way it had been when I found it. I set the carpetbag on the floor, grabbed the remote off the nightstand, and crawled in between the sheets. Surfing the channels, I hoped to find something I could get lost in. Passing on several talking heads, I finally settled on an old Orson Welles film noir movie that I'd never seen. Somewhere between the mysterious shadows and ominous and foreboding atmosphere, I must have fallen asleep.

sixteen

I ONCE WAS BLIND

I woke with my face buried in the down pillow and the Brahms's melody lingering in my brain. The morning sun had snuck in above the industrial-strength curtains, filling the room with a dull yellow light. Turning over, I saw that Maggie's bed was empty. I was in midstretch when I realized the music box melody wasn't inside my head at all, but playing somewhere nearby. I crawled out of bed, pulled my sweats on, and followed the sweet sounds to the bathroom door, which was slightly ajar.

"Maggie?" There was no answer.

I eased the door open with my foot, and there she sat, cross-legged on the brown fur rug and still dressed in her sleepwear. The music box was beside her, and fanned out on the cream-colored floor tiles in front of her lay all the black-and-white photos that Harvey had developed.

I'd been busted. Expecting to be bawled out, I braced myself. But Maggie didn't even acknowledge my presence. She just continued to stare down at the pictures. Maybe she was waiting for an apology.

"I'm sorry about the photos," I said. "I shouldn't have lied about it. I just didn't want you to make a big deal over them."

Maggie still didn't look up. Instead she reached out and ran her fingertips over the surface of one of the photos as if she were reading Braille. I didn't know what to make of it.

"You got it to work, huh? The music box, I mean," I said.

Maggie turned to the music box and touched the wings of the cherub on top. The tune abruptly ended. It made me feel more than a little uneasy. Still refusing to look up at me, she snatched up the photo she had been fondling and gently Frisbeed it in my direction. "You wouldn't let her kiss you, would you?" she asked.

I squatted down and picked up the photo of the little girl wearing the sunglasses and puckering her lips.

"Her name is Sheena," Maggie said in a whisper.

I stared at the picture . . . and remembered. The little girl lived three doors down from me when I was about six years old, and yes, her name *was* Sheena. How could Maggie possibly know?

"What's going on, Mags?"

Maggie continued to gaze at the assortment of photos. "The girl's name is Sheena, isn't it?" she asked, finally looking up at me for confirmation. Her eyes were red and tear filled.

I nodded. I wanted to walk away right then and there.

"These photographs . . ." she continued, "it's as if I were there—"

"You know, the sun's coming out," I began.

"—walking through this field, climbing on—"

"Hopefully they've cleared the tracks or opened the road so we can—"

"Did you hear me, David?" Maggie said, with an edge in her voice. "These trees, this tree house . . . this little girl . . . They feel so familiar to me . . . as if I know them. As if they're part of me."

I didn't know what to think, why this was happening. I just wanted her bizarre behavior to stop. "Put them away, Maggie."

"The blur here on this photo — " she said, picking up another picture and gently rubbing her thumbs over it.

"Come on." I began to collect the photos. "We can both just go home now. It's over. Roger and all, we're done with it."

"It's a dog," she said. "Long-haired, a retriever of some sort — "

"Stop!" I finally yelled. "This is ridiculous."

She closed her eyes, her voice cracking. "It's her dog, David. You know that, don't you? His name is Sam, or . . . sun-something."

She was leading me into a nightmare, and I refused to go. "I'm not listening to this insanity anymore," I said, standing up and taking a step outside the door.

"He's got a squeaky rubber steak in his mouth. Sun . . . Sunshine! His name is Sunshine," Maggie said with certainty.

I stopped in my tracks.

"But *you* always liked to call him Sunny," she added.

I stood with my back toward Maggie, remembering how I had wished he were my dog. With my last ounce of resistance I asked, "Why should I listen to you?"

"Because I don't want to be alone in this."

The desperation in her voice turned me back around. Tears were streaming down her cheeks. "You remember, don't you?" she asked.

"Yes," I said with a nod, then wondered out loud, "But how do you?"

Beneath a clear early morning sky, Maggie and I followed our steely blue shadows down the partially shoveled sidewalk toward the restaurant. At Maggie's request the carpetbag hung from my hand. She had been silent ever since the bathroom episode. Since she hadn't offered me an explanation for her psychic-hotline routine, it felt like a stranger was walking beside me. There was a physical change in her, too — a stiffness to her usually fluid body motion. Every stride she took appeared cautious.

"The sunglasses were never meant for my vacation," she said almost reluctantly. "But now I know what they were for."

"What were they for?"

"Last night . . . while you were taking your shower . . . I was laying in bed watching TV, and I guess I dozed off. When I woke up . . ."

"What?"

"There was this light."

"What are you talking about? What kind of light?"

Maggie stopped and faced me. "The carpetbag was lying open on your bed." She took a deep breath.

"And?"

"There was this glow . . . this golden glow. It was coming from inside the bag. And it began slowly flooding out of the bag into the room . . . getting brighter all the time. At first it really scared me. I mean I couldn't even move, it scared me so much. And I called out for you, but you mustn't have heard me."

"No, I didn't hear anything."

"And after a few moments, I could feel a heat that it was giving off. And then, something about the light made me feel . . . okay . . . safe even. It was actually quite beautiful. I didn't want to look away. But it kept getting brighter and brighter until finally I had to grab the sunglasses off the nightstand and put them on."

I remembered finding the sunglasses on the bed. Maybe she wasn't making this up.

"David, it was almost as if it was alive . . . a living thing."

"Old James coming back to pay a visit to his carpetbag, maybe?" I suggested. I couldn't see any point in discussing this with a serious tone. "Or maybe it was Roger returning for his mistletoe."

Maggie ignored my comments and started walking again. I could see there was more to the story than she was willing to share.

"And then something even stranger happened."

I wasn't certain that was possible, but I was willing to indulge her. "What would that be?"

"As soon as I put on the glasses . . . I could feel . . . It did something to me, David. Something physiological."

"Sex? You had sex with old James while I was in the shower?" I expected Maggie to get mad at me, but she was too into her story.

"It washed over me. The light washed over me and then filled me up with this feeling. This wonderful, intense, pleasurable feeling, like nothing I've ever experienced before. It was a kindness and a peacefulness and a love I can't begin to describe. Then suddenly it simply extinguished itself—like someone turned off a light switch. And I was back in the dark with only the TV on, feeling sleepy. And when I woke up this morning I felt . . . enlightened. I pulled those photos out of your jacket like I knew they were going to be there."

"I'm guessing you just had a very weird dream. Maybe it had something to do with the hors d'oeuvres you had last night. Those crab cakes were pretty intense."

"It wasn't a dream," Maggie said with certainty.

"So why didn't you tell me about this when I got out of the shower last night?"

"Because I was so exhausted by the experience that I just fell asleep. Besides, I knew you wouldn't believe me."

"So what makes you think I believe you now?"

"Because today I know that there was a little blonde-haired girl in your life who was named Sheena who had a dog named Sunny, and yesterday I didn't." She stared at me with eyes that said, *You know I'm right.* "This information isn't for me," she said. "And it's not going away, David. I can help you figure it out."

"There's nothing to figure out. This bag, this whole trip . . . It's been about you and Roger. End of story." I was hoping that by saying it, it might make it true. "I used to know a girl named Sheena when I was young. She used to have a dog and a music box—so what?"

"So you need to remember more."

"I don't want to remember more," I said, as we approached the front of the diner. But the truth was I had a strong sense that there was more to be remembered. Bits and pieces from my childhood were coming together like letters in a ransom note. But I had just as strong a sense that I shouldn't give in to their demands.

"After I grab something to eat, I'm taking a bus to the next *real* town where I'm going to rent a car to drive home," I said. "You're welcome to join me. But you need to know this adventure is officially over right now. So here," I forced the bag into Maggie's arms. "It's all yours. I'm sorry I ever found this stupid thing." I took a step in the direction of the glass door of the diner.

"Maybe you didn't."

I turned back toward her. "What?"

"Maybe you didn't find the bag."

"You're suggesting that this has all been a fantasy—some kind of grand illusion?"

"No. I'm suggesting that maybe the bag found you." She looked down at the snow. "I don't know how I know this, David, but I know what you were really doing that night."

I felt like I was in one of those dreams where I'm the only one walking around naked and there are no clothes to be found. "I don't know what you're talking about."

Maggie stared at me with eyes that pleaded with me to come clean. "The night you found the bag . . ."

"Yeah, what about it?"

"I know why you were on the roof."

She couldn't possibly know, but I was certain she did. I could feel my throat getting all lumpy.

"It's okay," she said. She wouldn't stop staring at me with that familiar look of sympathy.

I wasn't sure why, but for the first time in my life, I welcomed it. I wasn't going to lie to her again. I tried to think of other things in order to dam up my emotions, but nothing came to mind.

Maggie took a step forward and wrapped me up in her arms. "It's okay that I know," she said. "Really, it's okay."

It didn't feel okay. It felt painful. Scary. Dangerous.

"There's a reason you found the bag. Just like there was a reason that you found me."

"I just want to go home," I whispered into her ear.

"You can't."

"Why not?"

She slid her cheek against mine until I could feel her warm breath in my ear. Softly as a breeze, she said, "Because the journey isn't over."

Maggie's words immediately turned prophetic as a shrill call cut through the quiet morning air.

"Help! Someone, please!" Ethan's mom was running up the sidewalk toward us. Out of breath, she desperately pleaded, "Please, come help. It's Ethan."

seventeen

BETRAYED BY THE BAG

Sidestepping the melting slush on the sidewalks, the three of us ran down to the corner and up to a small wooden church. It had once been white, but age and the elements had taken a toll. Three-quarters of the way up the steep tin roof, Ethan lay on his stomach, dressed in his bright red nylon snowsuit. He was motionless, his arms and legs spread out, forming a big X. The glider was teetering just above him and beyond his reach at the base of the bell tower.

The sun had melted any remaining snow on the roof, leaving the surface not icy, but still plenty slick. If Ethan were to lose his grip, there'd be nothing to stop his slide.

Out of breath, Arlene pleaded with me. "Please do something."

A tall, barren tree standing alongside the church had probably been Ethan's access to the roof. Deciding on a more feasible route, I called out, "Ethan, don't move."

With an adrenaline rush, I took my first step toward the church, the morning sun reflecting off the steeple and into my eyes. In that moment of blindness, I saw *the toy wooden airplane sail into the lush green leaves of a tree . . .* It was the same hallucination I'd seen before, and it made me feel nearly as dizzy as the time I'd blacked out in the snow. But I couldn't afford any such reaction now.

I ran toward the entrance of the church. *Sheena clutched her Raggedy Ann doll and raced ahead of me.*

I pulled open the front door, rushed into the church—and crashed into an old oak podium. Pews, tables, and chairs littered the sanctuary of the small, abandoned chapel. The sunlight through cracked stained-glass windows fell across me, changing the color of everything . . . even my frame of mind. *Sheena smiled my way.* To my left a flight of bare wooden stairs ascended into shadows. *Sheena scooted up the stairs with a giggle, climbing the wooden slats on the tree trunk that led to our tree house.* I sprinted up the stairs, *chasing after her.* I raced up a second flight of stairs doubling back up into an attic—spotted a trap door in the center of the ceiling—hastily unlatched it—shoved it open.

Sunlight blinded me, and in that white light, *Sheena stepped onto the small deck of the tree house.* I climbed up into the wooden tower and maneuvered around the rusted bell and the attached wheel. *Sheena climbed out onto the sturdy limb that held the tree house.*

Looking down over the side of the bell tower, I could see Ethan, still a frozen X about ten feet below me, straining to hold on.

"Ethan, stay right there. I'm coming to get you." I scrambled over the waist-high tower wall and held onto its railing with one hand while trying to gain a solid footing on the roof. *Sheena tiptoed farther out onto the limb toward the glider caught in the branches.*

"Be careful, David," Maggie shouted.

Ethan looked up at me and spoke softly as if not to upset his tentative grip on the metallic roof, "Could you get the plane?"

The glider had crash-landed only a couple feet from my foot. But my eyes were on Ethan. I reached out for his hand and came up short. I couldn't bend down far enough and still manage to hold onto the tower's frame, and letting go of the railing would send both of us sliding down the roof. So, holding on, I eased my body onto the roof and stuck out my foot in Ethan's direction, extending it as far as I could. *Sheena stretched out her arm to retrieve the glider in the tree.*

"Try to grab my foot," I called down to Ethan. Slowly, he lifted a rosy hand off the surface of the roof, and reached out as far as he could toward my tennis shoe. *Sheena plucked the glider out of the branches' grasp.* Ethan's fingers were no more than an inch away from my shoe when his body began to slide away from me. His small hands clawed at the aluminum, but he wasn't slowing down.

"Ethan!" his mom screamed out above the high-pitched metallic grind of his fingernails. His slide picked up momentum, and I couldn't watch. I closed my eyes and saw *Sheena lose her balance on the limb of the tree, her Raggedy Ann doll falling to the ground.* I opened my eyes. Ethan was nowhere in sight.

I don't remember the paramedics loading Ethan into the ambulance, or his mom asking us to follow them to the hospital. I only remember sitting next to Maggie in the back seat of a police car, trailing in the wake of the ambulance's blaring siren. Neither Maggie nor I spoke for miles. Finally I had more things in my head than I could contain.

"You'd think I'd forget the sound of it," I said.

"The sound of what?" Maggie asked.

"My mother's voice. You'd think I'd have forgotten it by now. But I can make up any sentence in my head and hear exactly what she would sound like saying it. 'Pretend it never happened,' she said."

"Pretend what never happened?"

"Sheena. I watched her fall from a tree while she was trying to retrieve my toy glider—just like Ethan was doing. She died." Maggie looked at me like she'd already heard the news. She took my hand. "I was eight years old. I'd just lost my best friend, and to deal with the grief my mom told me to forget it . . . so I did."

"She was wrong to tell you that."

I glared down at the carpetbag at our feet, half hoping it would disappear if I continued to do so, half believing it would. It had betrayed me. A simple gift that brought Ethan and me so much pleasure now stood to bring us both just as much misery.

Maggie didn't let go of my hand until we reached the hospital.

The small waiting room in the Willowbrook hospital smelled of coffee and plastic. I leaned back on the emerald green vinyl couch across from Maggie and Ethan's mom. The beige walls displayed large, modern floral art prints with enamel frames that matched the pastel flower petals. I wondered if some interior decorator made that choice in order to soothe the anxious families and friends of patients. And I wondered if it ever made even one iota of difference.

We had been waiting for what seemed like hours for confirmation on Ethan's condition. I'd read *Time* cover-to-cover and thumbed the latest *People*, learning more than I ever needed to know about Drew Barrymore.

"He's my only son," Arlene repeated every few minutes.

"I'm sure they're doing all they can," Maggie replied each time. I was surprised at how much comfort Maggie had become to a woman she had once frightened away with baggage-induced hysteria.

I picked the carpetbag up off the floor and strolled out the door and across the hall to a large window that overlooked a frozen pond nestled among the skeletons of birch trees. I set the bag down on the windowsill.

The pond made me think about the previous winter and how Jeremy and Kelly had asked for ice skates for Christmas. After they fell asleep on Christmas Eve, I spent a couple hours flooding our backyard with water from our garden hose. I sprayed out the water evenly, building up one layer of ice on top of the last, covering the dead grass completely until the icy surface shone like glass in the moonlight. And through it all, as I stood there bundled up, sipping a mug of hot cocoa Kathy had brought out for me, I kept envisioning Jeremy and Kelly's expressions on Christmas morning, when they'd wake to shiny new ice skates and step outside to their own private skating pond. By the time I put away the hose that night, I didn't need to see their reaction. I knew they'd be thrilled. And so on that frigid Christmas morning, I stayed inside the house as my children discovered the backyard magic on their own.

Now, as I looked out at the pond outside the hospital window, I regretted not seeing my kids' faces that morning. It was what I needed to remember just then.

I wished I had laced up my own skates and waited outside to take their hands, spin them around, and help them back onto their feet after they fell. All those Kodak moments of intimacy with Kathy, Kelly, and Jeremy that I had carefully, conveniently avoided over the years—I wanted them all back. I needed to find myself posed inside that family portrait.

I turned around and noticed a doctor entering the waiting

room. Arlene and Maggie stood up to greet him. There was a second that I considered joining them, but the truth was I didn't want to hear the news in case it was bad. Expressionless, the doctor spoke, and Ethan's mom broke down in Maggie's arms.

Anger rose up inside me. I cranked open a long vertical casement next to the main window, grabbed the carpetbag and shoved it out. I didn't bother to watch it fall. *No more gifts.* I turned and began walking down the hallway with no destination in mind except away from there. My paced picked up. I passed an old man parked in a wheelchair alongside the wall, passed families, doctors, patients, and nurses in motion until I was oblivious to everyone and everything except an exit sign with an arrow pointing left. I was almost running now. I cut the corner short and ran headlong into Santa Claus, sending both him and his red bag full of wrapped presents spilling onto the floor. An elderly woman dressed as Mrs. Claus and walking at his side had somehow avoided the collision.

"Oh, I'm sorry. Are you okay?" I asked the Santa. I retrieved his Santa hat off the tile floor. Mrs. Claus rushed over and squatted down next to her husband.

"Oh, dear, are you all right?" she asked.

He remained lying flat on his back, not moving. "I'm fine, really." He didn't look fine. I thought I'd probably broken his back, leaving him paralyzed for life.

I knelt down next to him. "I'm so sorry. Don't move. I'll grab a doctor."

"Nonsense, I'm fine." Santa reached his arms out above his stuffed belly for assistance. I grabbed his black Santa mitts and pulled him to his feet.

"I was just in such a hurry," I said. "It was all my fault. I'm sorry."

"It's okay." He took his Santa hat from my hand and pulled it down over his balding gray head. "Mrs. Claus and I were in a bit of a hurry ourselves."

"Are you sure you're all right, dear?" his wife asked, adjusting his beard. He nodded.

I collected the scattered presents from the floor and began to stash them back into his red velvet bag.

"Look, if there's anything I can do . . ."

"Well, as a matter of fact . . . we're running a little late. How are you at giving out gifts?"

I couldn't bring myself to answer. Instead I lifted the bag up over my shoulder.

Santa produced a green elf hat out of the pocket of his fur-trimmed jacket and handed it to me. "I'm Bill, and this is my wife, Audrey," he said.

"Nice to meet you. I'm David." I squeezed the hat onto my head.

"Perfect fit," Bill said, though I was sure it was cutting off circulation to my brain, and I'd be passing out in a matter of minutes. But then again, that could be a good thing. What had I gotten myself into? I'd just rid myself of one bag full of gifts, and now I was stuck with another. Maggie was probably wondering where I was; I should have been with her and Ethan's mom.

But then Harvey's parting words to me came to mind: *Just do something nice for the next guy you run into, and we'll be even.* I hadn't realized he was speaking in literal terms.

Bill adjusted his wire-rimmed Santa glasses, took Mrs. Claus by the arm, and led the way down the hall. We stopped in front of a room where a young nurse holding a tray full of hospital parapher-nalia was walking out. "Oh, hi," she said with a beautiful smile.

"Is this a good time?" Santa asked.

"Are you kidding? I told them you might be by."

"Oh, good," Santa said.

"They're going to love it," the nurse said. "Just the kind of medicine they need."

She walked back into the room announcing, "Somebody's here to see you."

Before I could hand Santa the bag, he ambled into the room with a jolly "Ho, ho, ho! Who do we have here?" I started to follow him in, but Audrey grabbed me by the arm.

"Give them a moment," she said. "We don't want to overwhelm the children."

"It's just as well," I said. "I'm a little nervous about trying to pass for an elf."

"Well, don't be. It's not about you." She was right, of course. "Just look into their eyes and you'll do fine."

"But what if we give them something they don't want?"

"Oh, he's already given them what they want. But just in case, we do a little research beforehand. You'll find the kids' names on the presents. Don't worry. You'll do just fine."

From inside the room we could hear Santa say, "Presents? I don't know if I brought any."

"That's our cue," Mrs. Claus said.

I followed Mrs. Claus into the room carrying the bag of presents over my shoulder. In each of the two beds there was a young boy with a broad smile and excited look. One was hooked up to an IV; the other was thin and very sickly.

"Oh, now I remember," Santa said. "I did bring some presents after all."

"And I'll bet there's one in this bag for each of you boys," Mrs. Claus said.

"Have you ever met my wife, Mrs. Claus?" Santa asked the kids. They shook their heads. "She's a good woman. You'll like her. This is Justin and Blake."

"Hi, boys," Mrs. Claus said.

"And this guy," Santa said, pointing at me. "Who do you think he is?"

"I don't know," one of the boys said.

"Well, I'll tell you who he isn't. He isn't an elf. He's about twice the size of one of my elves, and take a gander at those ears of his. They don't even come to a point. Ho, ho, ho! Who's he kidding, right? He wears that hat like he's an elf, and he may tell you he's an elf, but don't let him fool you, okay? But he is here to dig your present out of my bag. Aren't you?" he asked me.

"Absolutely," I said. I began searching the bag for presents labeled "Justin" and "Blake."

For the next hour the three of us visited sick children and distributed gifts. After we had given away the first several presents, I began feeling at ease with the process. I actually looked forward to entering the next room, seeing the next face, and handing out the next gift. Mrs. Claus was right about looking into their eyes. They'd open their presents, and it never seemed to matter what was inside. Their happiness came from knowing that someone had given them something for no other reason than it was Christmas, and they were special.

eighteen

GOD'S GRACIOUS GIFT

The paper cup jiggled down into place. Steaming cocoa poured into it as I leaned up against the vending machine in the hospital's small, first-floor cafeteria. I looked out a nearby window and couldn't believe it was getting dark already.

Relaxing at a nearby table with Audrey, Bill removed his Santa hat, brushed a shock of hair over his dome, and sipped his coffee. "Thanks for your help, David. We really appreciate it."

"You're welcome."

There was something special about this couple. It wasn't simply their compassion for those sick kids that I found both admirable and contagious. I felt a connection that went beyond that. Their presence in my life at that moment gave me a feeling of calm, even though I knew that somewhere in that hospital Ethan's fate was still uncertain.

With the exception of a few workers shuffling around behind the food counter and one old woman cleaning off tables, the cafeteria was empty. I eased my hot cocoa out of the dispenser. "Handing out presents like that . . . Is it something you two do every year?"

"We have for some time now," Audrey said. She looked over at her husband and gave him a contented smile. "Haven't we, dear?"

"It's something we needed to do," said Bill. "You see, we lost one of our daughters when she was young." He picked up the empty red velvet bag off of the chair next to him and began to methodically fold it up on his lap. "She was a real firecracker, that one . . . high spirited, smart, athletic . . . but maybe more than anything, she was generous. And Christmas . . . well, Christmas was her favorite time. Like all kids, she liked to get presents, but giving them — that was something she truly loved to do." He set the neatly folded bag in front of him on the table and leaned back in his plastic chair.

Audrey stroked his shoulder. "When our daughter died," she began, "we didn't want that generosity to die with her, so we started raising funds in her name. Some presents are donated directly; others we purchase with financial contributions."

"The kids really seem to enjoy it," I said. "It's very good of you." I took a sip of my cocoa.

"Well, as I'm sure you could see, we get as much satisfaction out of it as the children do," said Bill. "I know it's the kind of thing that would have given great pleasure to Sheena."

I was sure I must have heard them wrong, yet my heart started pounding like crazy just the same. I slowly sat down across the table from Bill.

"I'm sorry . . . What was your daughter's name?"

"Sheena." He peeled his Santa beard off across his face and set it on the table. He didn't look familiar. "It's Irish," he said. "It means 'God's gracious gift.'" He scratched at his flushed cheeks.

Maybe it was a coincidence. I considered the odds. There had to have been at least a few other girls named Sheena who died when they were little, didn't there? A closer look at Audrey revealed nothing. This couple—their first names, their faces—they weren't familiar. This was certainly a different Sheena. It had to be.

To be absolutely positive, all I had to do was ask one question. It would even be appropriate under the circumstances: *How did she die?*

"David?"

I turned around, and Maggie was standing at the next table over, holding onto that lousy bag, snowflakes melting on its tapestry skin.

"There you are. I've been looking all over for you," she said.

"Maggie." I stood up and walked over to her.

"I even looked outside for you," she said, glancing down at the bag.

"You've rescued the enemy," I said.

She didn't respond. I wanted to ask her about Ethan.

"He's going to be okay," she said, as if she'd read my mind.

"But I saw his mom with the doctor—the way she broke down, I thought—"

"Arlene was very relieved. Ethan's regained consciousness. Except for a broken arm and a bump on his head, he's going to be fine."

"Hi, I'm Audrey."

At my side Audrey was holding out her hand to Maggie.

"I'm sorry," I said, "Maggie, this is Audrey."

"Hi," Maggie said.

Audrey smiled at Maggie, shook her hand, and they both held on as if this were a reunion of old friends. "It's very nice to meet you, Maggie."

"And this is her husband, Bill."

"Hello," Bill said with a wave. He scooted his chair away from the table and began to stand.

"Oh, please, don't get up," Maggie said with a smile. "With Christmas only a couple days away, Santa needs all the rest he can get. Nice to meet you both."

"Maggie's been my traveling companion the last few days," I informed them.

"Oh," Audrey said. "Well, I hope you don't mind that we borrowed him for a while." She fixed her gaze on the carpetbag.

"David was helping us distribute some gifts to the kids," Bill said.

"Gifts seem to be his specialty of late," Maggie said.

Audrey couldn't take her eyes off the carpetbag. "That bag. It's very unique . . . very unusual, isn't it?"

"Very," Maggie agreed.

"What I mean is . . ." Audrey looked at Bill, as if asking for his help.

He was already eyeing the bag. "May I take a closer look at it?"

Maggie walked over to the table and set the carpetbag down in front of Bill. I sat down across from him. He was staring it down, as if he were waiting for it to flinch. His attention was so focused on the bag that I, too, was drawn in to the contest.

I looked deep into the floral pattern—the mixture of faded burgundies, dusty roses, and smudges of olive.

"Do you remember, dear?" Audrey asked Bill, gently laying her hand on his.

"I do," he said softly.

It was almost as if I could feel my fingers running against the nap of the carpet without actually touching it. Was it just that I had come to know the look of this bag so well over the last few days, or was it something else? Suddenly it seemed so familiar. It was magnetic; I couldn't look away. The contempt I had been feeling for the bag began to fade.

"Our daughter used to have an old carpetbag that looked a lot like this one," Bill said. "Just like this one."

"Sheena and a friend found it out by the railroad tracks near our first house," Audrey said. "It was filled with some clothes and some odds and ends."

I stared at the gray shoelace looped around the handle. Frayed at both ends and tied in a knot around the brass key, it was a replacement. I was sure of it. The thin leather strap once attached to the key had worn off to be replaced by a shoelace from my own pair of Keds.

"Sheena and the boy down the block," Audrey continued, "they used to collect toys and knickknacks of all kinds in that old bag."

My brain screamed out to me. *I was that boy.* These *are* Sheena's parents. These are . . . *the McGuires.* That time and place more than thirty-five years ago came alive inside me, filling me with both joy and trepidation.

From behind me I felt Maggie's hands lightly press down on my shoulders.

"I don't know whatever happened to that bag," Audrey said, laying her hand on the top of it.

Maggie's fingers began to gently knead my knotted shoulder muscles.

"I can't get over how much this one looks like it," Audrey said. "Sheena and her friend kept it up in a tree house that Bill made for our kids. It was from that same tree . . . that she fell."

Maggie sat down next to me and asked Audrey, "I hope you

don't mind if I ask, but how did it happen?"

I turned away, hating her for asking.

"We weren't there," Bill said. "The boy was with her, though."

I couldn't stand it. I slipped out of my chair and walked over to the window and looked out at a parking lot.

"Yeah. He saw it all happen," Audrey added.

I could feel her eyes staring at the back of my neck; the anxious heat of it spread out across my shoulders.

"It was a hot summer day," Audrey said, "near the end of June. . . . They were playing with a toy airplane, one of those wooden wind-up kinds. And apparently it flew into the tree, got stuck in the high branches." Her voice was changing. She wasn't just telling the story, she was reliving it. And so was I. "Sheena was trying to retrieve the plane when . . . she must have just slipped, lost her balance. If she just hadn't been so high up . . ."

I could see Audrey's reflection in the window. She slid the carpetbag over in front of her as she stood at the table. Maggie was looking my way. Bill was leaning forward on the table, his head in his hands.

"What ever happened to the boy?" Maggie asked.

I knew what had happened to the boy, and now suspected why. My stomach was beginning to feel queasy.

"It's funny," Audrey said. "Bill and I were just talking about that very thing — it couldn't have been more than three nights ago. I had fallen asleep, and he woke me up. He said he couldn't sleep — that he wanted to talk about that boy. Do you remember, dear?"

Bill buried his face deeper into his hands.

Audrey continued to stare at the top of the bag. "I thought it was the oddest thing — right out of the blue. And so we sat up and talked about it . . . about how we were so wrapped up in our own grief after Sheena died that we never thought about the boy, never considered how he must have felt."

I was going to be ill.

Audrey slowly spread open the top of the bag. "After the boy's family moved away, we always regretted not telling him that we didn't blame him for what happened. It was simply the day"—Audrey opened up the bag and peered down into it. She saw something, something that weakened her voice—"Simply the day that the Lord chose to take our daughter."

I wanted to run—sprint out of the room, fly down the hallway, and burst through the glass doors out into the night.

"It wasn't his fault," Audrey said. "I hope he knows that."

The hum of the vending machine seemed to grow louder, until I couldn't stand it any longer. I had to escape.

"David?" Maggie called out softly.

I turned around and took off running past the three of them, out the door.

"Hey—wait!"

Sprinting down the hall, I turned the first corner crashed into a woman wearing scrubs.

"Oh, no—do you need some help?" she asked, but I didn't stop.

I found the front doors, ran outside. I fell down on my knees next to a bush and vomited until there was nothing left.

"David!" Maggie rushed over to me. She was holding the bag. I took a handful of snow and crammed it into my mouth, smearing the rest of it on my face. I spit out a mouthful of slush.

"Are you all right?" she asked.

I got to my feet and began running through the parking lot toward the highway. Maggie chased after me.

"Please, stop!"

I didn't. I couldn't get far enough away from her, the bag, and those memories. A car backed out of its parking space in front of me, slowing me down long enough for Maggie to catch up.

"Hey! What's wrong? They *forgave* you!"

"They weren't there. They didn't see." I made my way around the car and headed toward the highway.

Maggie continued the chase. "See what? What didn't they see?"

I reached the two-lane highway and looked down the road for approaching cars.

"It wasn't anyone's fault, really. Please look at me."

I couldn't. Instead I stuck out my thumb as headlights approached. "You can't help me, Maggie. Please just go away." The cars roared past us.

"Look at me," Maggie said, grabbing my sleeve. I turned around and looked into her eyes. "Talk to me."

"I tried to tell her . . ." I began.

"Who? Who did you try to tell?"

"I tried to tell her that it was my fault, but she wouldn't listen."

"Who? Audrey?"

"She wouldn't listen to me. She just kept wiping away my tears and saying, 'It's okay, it's going to be okay. Just pretend it never happened.' She knew I was to blame. My mom knew."

Maggie dropped the bag and tried to embrace me, but I didn't want to be comforted. I broke away—turned around, and there at the side of the road in front of me was an old red pickup truck with the passenger door wide open. Beneath a dim cabin light, a faceless figure in a broad brimmed hat and fur coat sat hunched over the steering wheel. Strains of Patsy Cline's impassioned voice declaring her "Crazy" filtered out of the truck.

"Well, you need a lift or not?" the gravelly voice of an older woman asked. "Got places to be, you know."

I hesitated, but Maggie stepped in front of me and climbed into the front seat of the truck, leaving me no choice but to join her. She extended her hand and yanked me up into the cabin.

"Thanks for the ride," Maggie said to the woman.

"Sure 'nuff." The woman shifted into first, grinding out the gears until we jerked forward and began rolling down the road.

nineteen

GOING HOME

The truck smelled of damp sod. I leaned back on a Navajo blanket that was draped over the back of the seat. I felt somewhat relieved, but I didn't feel free.

"The name's Sophie. How far you goin'?"

"We don't even know the name of the town," Maggie said. "But there's this place not far from here—the Big Moose Inn."

"Gwynnie's place?" It was a confirmation, not really a question.

"Right," Maggie said.

"Oh, sure, I know it," Sophie said. "Well, you're in luck. I happen to be passing right through there."

Guilt was continuing to weigh me down when I realized something was different. I turned to Maggie. "The bag . . ." I began. "Where's the bag?"

"You don't have it?" she asked, looking around the floor.

I wasn't sure how to feel about leaving it behind. In a way I was happy to be done with it—the magic, the power the carpetbag held over us. It had taken me as far as it could. I was now finally setting my own course, and the destination clearly had to be *home*.

Still, it felt strange. It had forced me to remember the role it had played in my childhood. It had been our secret bag, holding the only important possessions of our private world.

As much as I didn't want to think about them, other memories of Sheena started coming to mind: collecting fireflies, playing spud and hide-and-go-seek all over the neighborhood, catching crayfish in the creek that ran through the field. I remembered riding our bikes to a fireworks stand with her older brother. And how when no one was looking, he stole a bunch of giant bottle rockets. He gave us one of them and told us not to blow ourselves up. Sheena and I were planning on setting it off on the Fourth of July, right there in the meadow. We never got the chance.

Every pleasant memory had the same unhappy ending. The hole of depression that I was falling into, deeper and deeper by the moment, had nothing to do with the bag and everything to do with the sense of losing Sheena for a second time, knowing that I was the reason she was gone.

I was the reason Audrey's voice still cracked when she spoke of the day her daughter died. I was the reason Sheena's dad had to hide his face in his hands when he heard the details of that day.

But Audrey was wrong: The Lord didn't choose to take their daughter that day. It was my doing, my carelessness, my selfishness that caused so many people so much pain.

"Looks like the storm's finally given up," Sophie said.

Heat was rising from the floor. Outside my window the night sky shone with a dim blue glow above a hilly horizon line, as if the moon were about to rise. I waited for it to show itself, wishing I could leap aboard and sail across the star-filled sky. But I couldn't. It wouldn't be fair. I deserved the memory of Sheena's death and the pain it brought. I owed it to Sheena to stay here and feel this agony. Her parents, her family, I owed it to them. I owed it to the friends she would have made growing up, and to the young man who was never given the chance to hold her in his arms, look into her blue eyes, and tell her that she was the love of his life. After all those years of denial, I now owed it to myself to take responsibility for what I'd done.

I must have fallen asleep because I opened my eyes to a full moon hanging halfway up the sky. The distant hills had been replaced by a housing tract just off the highway.

On the radio an unfamiliar country song faded into a buzz of bad reception. Sophie reached over and turned off the noise.

"Where are we?" I whispered with a yawn. Neither Maggie nor Sophie offered an answer. The clanging of a distant bell filled the dead air. I turned to find Maggie asleep, her head on my shoulder.

The truck dipped into a pothole. Maggie stirred, then sat upright.

Sophie downshifted and the belly of the truck let out a mournful whine.

"What time is it, anyway?" I asked. The horn from an approaching train provided the only response.

I could see that we were coming up on a line of braking taillights and, ahead of them, the flashing red lights of a railroad crossing. The warning bell sounded in rhythm to the passing train. "How long have we been driving?"

"I have no idea," Maggie said.

"But where are we?" I asked Sophie directly this time.

"'Fraid we might be in for a considerable wait," she replied.

Maggie stared out my window. "*I* know where we are."

"Where?"

"You don't know?"

"No. I have no idea—where?"

Maggie pointed out the window and I looked.

A snow-covered park with playground equipment was off to our right now. At the opposite end of the park was a group of trees. But that wasn't what Maggie was pointing at. Rising up above and beyond the gray mass of trees was what looked like a giant golf ball on an equally giant tee. Moonlight illuminated the letters on the face of the water tower just enough for me to make them out . . . G-L-E-N-V-I-E-W.

This had been my home for the first seven years of my life. I didn't recognize the park, but having regained my bearings, I knew that beyond those trees was the field where Sheena and I used to play. And a short distance from there was the house I grew up in. I hadn't been back since our family moved away. Even though I had completely lost track of where our travels had led us over the past couple days, it didn't seem possible that I could be back in Glenview.

Sophie stopped the truck. "I recollect near thirty-odd years ago some fool in a semi tried to beat one of these trains 'cross the track. Caused an awful mess."

I looked out past the park and began to remember.

"Derailed 'bout twenty cars," Sophie continued. "I forget how many people died that night."

I remembered waking to the terrible sounds of the crash on that hot summer night. My mom assured me it was nothing and settled me back to sleep with a song. It was weeks later that Sheena and I literally stumbled across the carpetbag lying hidden in the long grass.

The water tower wasn't as enormous as I remembered. I had

once climbed a third of the way up its side before losing my nerve and turning back.

The freight train streaked through the crossing, its horn screaming at us. I had the feeling it was the one waiting on me instead of vice versa. It was prepared to parade a zillion train cars past me until I finally made a move to confront my past.

So I opened the door and climbed out of the truck into the glare from the headlights of the cars lined up behind us.

"David, where are you going?" Maggie asked.

Taking a step off the highway, my tennis shoes sank through a layer of ice into a foot of snow.

"Wait," Sophie called out.

I turned around and saw Sophie pull out an old wooden shovel with a metal handle and blade. She passed it to Maggie.

"What's this for?" Maggie asked.

I wasn't sure myself. I only knew that I'd be needing it. Apparently it had been lying beside the heater, because as I took it from Maggie, I could feel heat rising off the blade. I turned and began trudging through the field of snow toward a grove of bare maples covered with blue frosting.

"What's the shovel for?" Maggie called out. She jumped out of the truck. "You're not planning on digging someone up, are you?"

Walking under a street lamp and past a jungle gym, I picked up my pace, anxious to prove to myself that this particular Glenview wasn't some sort of Brigadoon—or a mirage like Elizabeth's bedroom had been. I left the park behind, entering the shadows cast by the trees. The low rumbling of train cars and the clanging railroad crossing signal subsided to be replaced by the sound of a second set of footsteps crunching in the snow behind me.

"David!" I spun around. Twenty feet away, Maggie stood bent over, her hands on her knees, trying to catch her breath. I walked back to her. She reached out her hand, and I took it. Together we entered the woods.

We made our way through the small, dense grove of maples. Lights from nearby houses on our left strobed through the web of branches as we walked. The tree line ended, and we entered an open field of snow glistening in the moonlight. A large oak stood naked in the middle of the meadow—like it owned the place.

"This is it, isn't it?" Maggie asked. "The photographs—this is the place, right?"

Still carrying the shovel, I walked toward the tree, Maggie following. I stood beside its ancient, mammoth trunk and looked up at its countless branches. There on one of the lower limbs was a narrow, two-foot-long weathered board waiting to greet me. It had held on by a single nail, season after season, until I finally showed up. It was the last remnant, the only indication that a tree house once resided there. I almost expected the board to suddenly fall to the ground in front of me, having served its purpose.

"This was the tree, wasn't it?" Maggie asked with joy in her voice, as thrilled as if she had once climbed upon it herself.

Now I knew what the shovel was for. With my back up against the trunk, I measured off ten kid-sized steps away from the tree in the direction of the water tower.

"What are you doing?" Maggie asked.

I thrust the shovel into the snow, and wisps of steam rose and quickly vanished. I began to clear away a two-by-two-foot area, until I uncovered long strands of dead grass. "After she died, I remember sitting up in that tree house by myself for hours, thinking that I never wanted to get that close to anyone again."

"But you do," Maggie said. "We all do."

I planted the shovel into the ground and jumped onto the blade. The shovel's head sank with surprising ease. I scooped up dirt and heaved it off to the side.

"All the while, that dog of hers sat at the base of the tree, looking up, whimpering, like he was just waiting for her to come down."

"David, don't—"

"I tore lives apart. Bill and Audrey have never—"

"They forgave you."

"I should have done something."

"What could you have done?"

My shovel struck something that made a hollow, wooden sound. "I don't know . . . something. I should have been the one to retrieve the glider when it got stuck in the tree, not her."

"She was a tomboy, wasn't she?" Maggie asked. "She probably scaled this tree in no time."

"When she walked out on the limb, holding that doll of hers . . . I tried to get by her but—"

"She wouldn't let you by."

"I should have found a way," I said.

"And when she grabbed the glider out of the branches—what happened?"

"She wouldn't give it to me."

I dug around the edge of rotting wooden planks. "But I never should have gotten angry—I just got so angry."

Maggie squatted down and looked up at me. "Why? Why did you get mad?"

"It was stupid. It was so stupid of me. It was my turn to fly the plane."

"And that's what upset you?"

"No."

"What then?"

"She laughed at me," I said. The wood splintered in several places as I tried to pry it up, revealing a hole underneath.

"She shouldn't have done that," Maggie said, as though she had witnessed the humiliation.

"Still, it was wrong for me to get angry. I didn't mean to hurt her—"

"I know. I know you didn't."

I fell to my knees and pulled away the scraps of wood and tossed them aside. "I just wanted her to stop making fun of me."

"She shouldn't have laughed at you."

"That doll—that stupid doll. She kept pushing it in front of my face and laughing. I shouldn't have tried to grab it from her. 'Cause when I did . . . I pushed her away . . . and then . . ."

"She lost her balance."

"We both did. But I grabbed a limb above me."

"You could have just as easily been the one who fell."

"I wish I had been."

Tears blurred my vision as I reached into the damp hole with both hands and eased the carpetbag out of the ground. The bag was cold and wet and covered with mud.

"She was my friend," I said. "My first friend."

I set the bag down in the snow. My thumb pressed against the latch above the keyhole. The bag clicked open. Nothing felt magical about this bag. It was lifeless, full of death. I spread apart the top, turned it upside down, and out onto the snow tumbled the box camera, the copy of *Green Eggs and Ham*, the rubber snake, the sunglasses, the cameo brooch, the dog's rubber steak chew toy, the music box, the Cracker Jack ring, the airplane, the autographed baseball, the Raggedy Ann doll, the train tickets, and the white feather. I covered my face, bent over, and began to cry.

Maggie placed her hand on my shoulder. "It's going to be okay."

"No, it's not. Don't you see—it's never going to be okay again."

"You've haven't been brought here to be condemned for what happened, but to be free of it."

"I can never be free of this."

Maggie took hold of both my shoulders and squared them off. "Look at me." I looked up at her. "Remember that night . . . that night on the rooftop . . ."

"When?"

"When you first saw the bag. You were on the ledge, and you had been angry and you cursed God. . . ."

"You don't know that—you can't."

"You cursed him for your rotten life . . . but then you asked him for something. Remember?"

"No, I don't remember."

"Think about it, David."

"No. I don't want to think about it."

"You blamed him for your life, but then you asked him for something . . . what was it?"

I remembered. Desperate words whispered to the heavens.

Maggie moved in closer. "What did you ask him for?"

"It's not that simple."

"In that very moment, he forgave you—just like Sheena's parents. He forgave you."

"I was the reason she fell. Don't you see—I don't deserve to be forgiven."

Maggie took hold of my hands. "But you are. The one thing you two shared . . . this bag . . . your connection with her. It brought you here for that very reason."

"You don't understand," I said.

"This stuff, these memories, these . . . gifts for strangers . . . but now, this is your gift, David. This resolution . . . your restoration. You need to open your heart. Let yourself receive it through grace. Let it begin to change your life."

"You don't understand . . ." I began.

"I do."

"It was my fault. It was my doing." A warmth began to emanate from Maggie's hands. "No one can change that," I said.

Maggie's deep green, sympathetic eyes began to lighten; they were almost luminous.

"But you are forgiven," Maggie said.

"No. Don't you see? There's only one person who could have ever forgiven me."

Maggie stared into my eyes, and slowly leaned toward me, her cheek sliding up along side of mine. She whispered into my ear with the voice of a child, "Davy, I do forgive you."

As she kissed my cheek, an astonishing burst of heat and light exploded in front of me. I fell back onto the snow, turning my face away from the brilliance. In a matter of moments the intensity subsided. When I sat up, there in Maggie's place stood a young girl dressed in yellow Bermuda shorts and a T-shirt, her long blonde hair in a ponytail. It was Sheena. Her image remained just long enough for her to smile at me, only long enough for the shame and guilt that had consumed me to dissipate. Her face began to radiate with a glow that quickly spread to her entire body, intensifying into an incredible white light, impossible to view. I turned away.

In an instant the light was gone, and once again Maggie was sitting in front of me, her chin resting on her chest. As she slowly raised her head, I could see cheeks streaked with tears on a face completely at peace. We both sat silently in the snow for a good minute, feeling physically drained, emotionally spent, sensing a completion of our journey. I opened up the top of the bag to pack up its contents. An object sparkled at the bottom. I reached in and pried out something long and thin, wrapped in aluminum foil.

"What's that?" Maggie asked.

I pulled back the foil. Inside was a giant bottle rocket. Its paper covering of red and blue stars and stripes was only slightly water damaged.

"What is it?" Maggie asked.

I took the rocket out of the foil and handed it to Maggie. She looked it over and then crammed its red stick base into the frozen snow, its nose pointing toward the moon. She extended her hand toward me, palm up.

"What?" I asked.

"Matches?"

"I don't have—" But then I remembered. I reached into my pocket and pulled out the book of matches that John had given me. I slid open the cover to reveal one remaining match. I looked over at Maggie and she smiled. We huddled together against the mild breeze. I ripped the match from its book, struck it once, cupped my hands around its dancing flame, and held it under the rocket's three-inch-long black fuse. Nothing happened. The flame nearly flickered out. Still nothing. The match flame crawled toward my fingers until finally I could barely detect a glow at the tip of the fuse. The match burned out. The glow spit out a couple sparks, then a flurry of them, then a small ball of sparks ignited and began to climb up the fuse.

With a cry of excitement, Maggie jumped up, grabbed my arm, and we backed away. The sparks made contact with the bottom of the rocket, sputtered, then burst into a red flame, shooting the rocket straight up into the cold, dark sky with a screaming whistle and a fiery tail. Soaring far beyond the top of the tree, it exploded with a loud pop, bursting into a small shower of sparkling diamonds against the night sky.

twenty

A CALL FROM
MR. COOPER

I wasn't certain what to do with the carpetbag. The remnants of my childhood couldn't remain buried, and I knew they couldn't come with me either. Disposing of the bag in a dumpster didn't seem appropriate, and neither did giving it away, not that anyone would be in the market for any of the junk. Even the Babe's signature had been transformed over the years into a worthless ink blur.

So I left the carpetbag in the care of the oak tree, laying it beside the great trunk, certain the tree would know what to do with it.

"May I keep the Cracker Jack ring?" Maggie asked me before we left. I wasn't sure why she wanted it, but I told her, "Fine with me."

By sheer luck—or was it?—we easily found our way back to Chicago. It was Christmas Eve, though it certainly didn't feel like it. On the trip home, we talked about our journey until there was nothing left to say on the subject of mystical carpetbags, miracles, and forgiveness. There was some talk of getting together once in a while for a friendly drink—to remind each other that we weren't delusional. And Maggie persuaded the New York publisher to give her another shot at an interview—after Christmas.

In the cab on our way from the train station, she said, "I was thinking about Peter and Roger."

"What about them?"

"Remember what Peter said to me after we'd danced together?"

"I remember it being a little odd."

"He said that he would have understood if I had been too afraid to dance with him. No, actually, *awkward* was the word he used—'if I felt too awkward.' He said something about how difficult it could be to take a chance. But he said he understood if I couldn't. Then he called me Margaret. Roger always called me Margaret."

At last she understood the reason for Roger's return. And I understood, too, that Maggie had traveled the same road as me . . . for the same reason.

I walked Maggie up to her second floor apartment, intending to say good-bye at her door. Last count, we had unsuccessfully said farewell to each other four times over the last four days. This one was going to stick. But before I had a chance to speak, she pushed open her apartment door.

"Why don't you come in for a while?"

"Why would you want to spend even more time with me?"

She took my hand and pulled me into the living room. I couldn't help but feel the big bump on her finger. I took one last look at the Cracker Jack prize pinched around her pinky.

"Why did you want that thing, anyway?" I asked.

"Oh, I don't know . . . I guess I just wanted something to remember Elizabeth by . . ."

"I can understand that," I said.

". . . and something to remember her fiancé by, too." She reached out and hugged me, an act we had come to perfect. "Maybe she was right about you."

"Who?"

"Kathy. The lousy thing she said about you that night." She slowly broke away. "Maybe she was right about you back then, but she isn't now. Make sure she knows that."

I wanted to tell Maggie how much she'd meant to me over these past few days—how reaching that destination would never have been possible without her. "I just want you to know . . . " I began.

The phone on the kitchen wall began to ring. Maggie ignored it. "I do," she said, with a smile.

The phone rang a second time. "Can I get you something to drink?" she asked.

"No, thanks. I should be going."

The phone rang a third time.

"Aren't you going to answer that?" I asked.

"Whatever they're selling, I'm not interested." Maggie took off her coat. "Are you sure you can't stay awhile?"

"No, there's things I need to do. You know."

The answering machine picked up. The deliberate voice of a nervous man spoke. "Hello, Maggie. You probably didn't expect to hear from me again after my no-show at the restaurant . . ."

Maggie and I both turned our attention to the phone.

Bigzaney4 continued, "I called you several times over the last few days to apologize. Shoot—I didn't want to have to go the chicken's route and leave you a message . . . okay, here goes . . . I just wanted to say I'm sorry. Any way you look at it, it was wrong of me. The truth is I did show up that night. . . ."

"Oh, great," Maggie said, disappointed.

"But when I saw you through the window, sitting there where you said you'd be, I couldn't go through with it."

"What did I tell you?" Maggie said.

"Your photo on your profile looked okay," Bigzaney4 continued, "but when I saw you in person . . . well, you were so . . . attractive. I mean you looked so fantastic that I immediately knew I was out of my league."

"See," I began, "you shouldn't have been so quick—"

"*Shhh.*" Maggie raised her hand to silence me.

"You see, I exaggerated a bit about my appearance," the phone voice continued. "I don't really look all that much like Gary Cooper like I told you . . . more like Alice Cooper, or my friend, Billy Cooper, who I realize you don't actually know, but take my word for it, he isn't the greatest looking guy in the world."

Maggie smiled at the floor.

"I mean I'm not ugly. I don't have, you know, horns growing out of my head or anything, but . . . What I'm trying to say in my own inept way is . . . I'm sorry it didn't work out. That's all I really called to tell you. So I hope we can still chat online sometime. Until then . . ."

It was as if the starter gun had gone off for the fifty-yard dash. Maggie sprinted across the room toward the phone. As Bigzaney4 said, "Good-bye," she ripped the receiver off the hook and slammed it up against her ear.

"Hello? Hello?" she said frantically. A relieved expression took over her face. "Yes, no, I just walked in. . . . No, no, I just caught the very end of it. You'll have to repeat it for me."

Maggie looked my way and smiled. I waved good-bye. She blew me a kiss.

I left Maggie's apartment knowing that I wouldn't be seeing her for a while. But I also knew that we would be forever linked by an extraordinary few days, and that one day we would feel the need to get together over a drink, if for no other reason than to reassure ourselves that it all really happened.

When I entered my apartment, I was immediately hit with the putrid smell coming from the trash can in the kitchen. As I tied up the top of the trash bag to take it outside, I noticed a paper plate on my kitchen table; the words *TONIGHT—TRIM TREE—7:30* were scribbled across it in bold black marker. It seemed as though I had written that note to myself a lifetime ago. I wondered whether, had I managed to obey that reminder, my life might have played out differently over these past few days.

Exhausted from the trip, I decided to give my body a break. Lying on my back on the bed, I stared up at the ceiling, my arms to my sides. A white muslin curtain covered the window to my right. I could feel the room slowly filling with dusk. It felt nice. Aside from an occasional car passing and a dog barking in the distance, the room was wonderfully serene.

I thought about what Maggie had said just before "the miracle" occurred. I wondered if a change had actually taken place inside me. I tried to sense one. I wasn't even sure how to go about sensing a change, so I waited patiently to feel something different, certain that if I tried hard enough, I would.

My mind began to wander. I started thinking about the damage my mom had done when she advised me to forget the incident. From that day on I had stuffed those feelings of heartache and self-blame so deep within me that they appeared to be gone.

What I didn't realize was that I'd crammed part of me in there with them — the part of me that could feel, the part that could be passionate about anything. It altered how I related to every human being I came in contact with.

Maybe I should have felt angry toward my mom, resentful for how she behaved in the face of my personal anguish over Sheena's death. But she had acted the only way she knew how: like a parent. Being a parent myself, I could understand her position. Her only wish at that time was to end my misery and to absorb my suffering herself. She did the wrong thing for the right reason. How could I possibly be angry with her for that?

I rolled over onto my side toward my nightstand. The message light on the telephone was glowing red. Unaccustomed to getting many messages, I hadn't even bothered to check it. I propped myself up on my elbow. The phone indicated that I had four messages — breaking the old record by three. I pressed the Play button. A mechanical woman gave me the day and the time of the call, followed by a man's voice.

"Mr. David Connors, you've been selected to be our guest for a three day getaway at the — " I pressed the Skip button. After the mechanical woman came on again, I heard a familiar voice.

"David, this is Kathy. Give me a call." Though she sounded even less enthusiastic than the mechanical woman, it was still good to hear her voice. I was surprised to hear it again on the third message.

"David, this is Kathy again. . . ." I could already tell that she was upset about something. "You never returned my call. The kids wanted me to remind you that the Christmas pageant is this Saturday night at seven thirty. It would be nice if you decided to show up. That's all. Bye."

The fourth message was also from Kathy.

"I stopped by your apartment last night. Your neighbor — the one that's always wearing the purple bathrobe — he said he hadn't seen you or your car in a couple of days." There was a long pause. "I hope everything's okay. Please give me a call."

There was a genuine concern in Kathy's voice. I felt a stirring in my chest. It might have been my arteries clogging up, but I preferred to believe that it was a new heart condition — a souvenir that I brought back from my vacation to Glenview.

twenty-one

THE SPACE
BETWEEN US

I was reminded that I had arrived early to the Christmas pageant when I pulled into the church parking lot and found a choice space along the side of the building. I got out of my car, scanned the lot for Kathy's Accord, and spotted it across the way. Seeing it made me nervous, a nice nervous. Maybe it was a good thing that I couldn't reach her on the phone earlier. Now I could see the concern on her face firsthand. Distant voices in song floated on a cold breeze from around the corner of the church.

I tracked those voices to the front where a group of two men and two women, dressed in formal Victorian garb harmonized a cappella. Bundled up in their overcoats, top hats, bonnets, mufflers, and muffs, they sang "We Wish You a Merry Christmas" beneath an old-fashioned streetlamp. Watching them gave me the first real sense that Christmas was here. It felt good.

I paid for a pageant ticket at a nearby card table and walked up the stairs into the church.

Inside the small foyer a little boy and girl, also in Victorian attire, stood on either side of the doorway handing out programs. I received one from the shiny-shoed boy; he was wearing a permanent grin, obviously enjoying the responsibility usually reserved for adults.

Dimmed lights hanging from the vaulted ceiling lit up the sanctuary. It was filled with holiday decorations and alive with the murmur of early arrivals visiting in and around the pews.

I paused at the back of the room to look for Kathy, letting others stream past me down the middle aisle in search of good seats. How could I possibly explain to Kathy where I'd been and how I'd gotten there? When we last saw each other outside her classroom, I'm quite sure she thought I was a complete madman. But after having survived the lunacy of the past few days, I now felt saner than I ever had before.

"David . . ." A smiling usher approached me with his hand extended.

I recognized him but couldn't remember his name. Kathy and I had gone out to dinner with him and his wife, Sally, a couple years back. I remembered what I ate that night—lemon chicken and a Caesar salad—but his name eluded me.

"How are you?" he asked.

"Good, good," I replied. Halfway through a vigorous handshake, I noticed the small nametag on his lapel.

"Merry Christmas," he said.

"Merry Christmas to you, Bruce," I replied, impatiently rolling up my program like a diploma. I just wanted to see Kathy.

"Sally tells me Jeremy's got a starring role in the play. Gabriel, no less, huh?"

"That's what I hear," I said. "Have you seen Kathy by any chance?"

"Oh, yeah, she's right up front there—can't miss her."

"Great. Thanks." I started backing down the aisle. "Good seeing you."

"Good to see you again, David. Enjoy the show."

With a wave and a nod, I turned and continued slowly toward the front of the sanctuary. A lightweight purple curtain was strung across the front of the stage. A small orchestra made up of three strings, three horns, a percussionist, and a pianist was tuning up, stage right.

In the third row, one seat from the aisle, Kathy sat wrapped up in her gray, bulky knit turtleneck. I wanted to fall on my knees and apologize to her, to say I was sorry for the space I'd placed between us over the years. But she'd heard that song before—those hollow apologies that had never resulted in my changing a bit.

I walked up beside Kathy's pew while she was visiting with an older woman on her far side. I could smell Kathy's unmistakable scent. Shampoo? Perfume? Body lotion? A combination? I wasn't sure and didn't care—it just was nice to be in the presence of her aroma again.

Her voice had sounded so sweet and full of concern on that last phone message. I wondered if now, seeing me in person, she'd make a scene, leaping up to embrace me, maybe even giving me a kiss.

"Kathy?"

She didn't hear me.

I touched her shoulder. She turned around toward me. "David! Where the h—where have you been?"

She was so upset that she nearly used a word I've never heard her say except, of course, when referring to the place in which she'd always suggested I'd be spending eternity. This was not the kind of scene I was hoping for; every head within earshot jerked in our direction.

"What?" I said, stunned at her reaction.

"Didn't you get my messages?" I swear I saw flames shoot from her eyes.

"Well, yeah, I did, but—"

"Then why didn't you return my calls? The least you could have done—"

"Wait," I said, trying to calm and quiet her down. She was so upset with me that it had taken her this long to realize we had an audience. She turned to the lady next to her and said politely, "Excuse me."

Kathy slid out of the pew and walked down the aisle past the front row and turned right in front of the orchestra. I dodged a sliding trombone and followed her through a side door that led up four steps toward the backstage area. She stopped at the top of the stairs.

"Why didn't you return my calls?" she asked again. Ahead of us we could see the kids in costume milling around their teachers.

Kathy opened a door to our left and pulled me into a small enclosed landing that led several steps down to a baptismal tank. I closed the door behind me. Backlit by the house lights, short curtains hung across the window at the far end of the tank, closing off the room from the congregation. Kathy turned to me. "Well?"

"I didn't return your calls because I just got the messages a couple hours ago."

"This is just like you, David, so inconsiderate! You just show up out of the blue—"

"You didn't want me to show up?"

"Of course I did! But you disappear for several days without a word and then suddenly pop up, and you're wondering why I'm mad?"

"I'm really sorry."

Kathy sat down on the top step, facing the small pool of water. I slid down against the wall to my left, next to her on the narrow stairway.

"When you showed up at school, acting so strange, carrying around that weird bag, I got worried about you."

"You still care about me?"

She sighed. "Of course I do. When you didn't return my calls, I thought maybe you had done something crazy, you know? And I don't care if you like this or not, David, but I've been praying for you ever since. So please give me the consideration of telling me where you've been."

I looked down at the program in my hand and unrolled it. On the cover was a simple black-and-white sketch of the three wise men following the bright star in the east. I wanted to tell Kathy the complicated truth: that a carpetbag had led me on an incredible journey and possibly changed my life.

"I can't tell you."

"Why do I do this to myself?" Kathy shook her head. "All week I had this feeling . . . but you haven't changed. Nothing's changed. I must be crazy. Fine, just be your usual evasive self." She turned away from me.

"I can't tell you where I've been because you wouldn't believe me."

"Why not?"

"Because I barely believe it myself."

"Trust me; at this point, you have nothing to lose." She glared at me.

I stared down at the water. Though the room was dark, I was still able to see the glassy golden reflection of the curtains on the water.

Just over a year ago I'd sat, at Kathy's request, on the other side of those curtains in the congregation and watched Pastor Neal baptize her and the kids in that same tank. It had been nearly unbearable to listen to Kathy give her testimony as she stood waist high in the water that Sunday morning. She talked about how messed up her life had been and how unhappy she had become. And when she told the congregation how she could feel Christ molding her and changing her life for the better, she looked straight at me. I knew now that it was meant to be a look of encouragement, but back then it felt like a look of blame. I remembered how I'd had to look away.

"I now baptize you in the name of the Father, the Son, and the Holy Spirit," the pastor had said. I could hear the splash as Kathy was fully submerged into the water. I looked back and watched her resurface to the overwhelming, supportive applause.

Though it wasn't one of eternal salvation, I realized that I had a testimony of my own to present. I only hoped Kathy wouldn't turn away as I had done.

So I began to stumble through my best *Reader's Digest* version of my odyssey. I explained to her how I'd found the bag on the ledge, how I met Maggie in the bar, and how the two of us were led on the journey together by the contents of the bag. I made it clear that my relationship with Maggie never moved past the friendship stage. Kathy sat calmly with her hands folded in her lap as I told her about the train trip and the camera, about Ethan and the glider, and everybody ending up in the Big Moose Inn. The more of the story I told, the less I believed it myself.

I babbled on about how the bag kept producing gifts that seemed strangely familiar to me, and how they managed to unblock my memory of my childhood friend, Sheena. Kathy listened intently, never interrupting, as I told her how I ran into Sheena's parents, and how Maggie and I were led to my hometown, where I dug up the bag and dumped out all the gifts.

I hesitated to finish the outrageous story, putting off the inevitable moment when Kathy would write me off as officially flipped out. But I proceeded, telling her how I was forced to remember Sheena's death, and how I felt it was my fault. At that point Kathy's demeanor softened, and she reached over and touched the sleeve of my coat in a gesture of consolation. I continued on to what I knew would be the most difficult part of the story for Kathy to accept. I explained how the image of Sheena momentarily materialized and forgave me for what I had done to her all those years ago.

I concluded with the obvious. "It was a life-changing experience."

Kathy took a deep breath. "I have a few questions," she said.

It wasn't just my character that was on trial, it was my sanity. "I'm sure you do. Go ahead."

"All these objects that you say suddenly materialized in that bag—they all had a purpose?"

"Yeah. They seemed to be what people needed."

"So what was the purpose of that little toy that you gave me?"

I thought about the wooden egg and came up empty. If I failed to answer her first question, my case was in serious trouble.

"I have no idea," I confessed.

"You said that when you dug up the bag, all those toys and

things that you had given away were there in the bag—right?"

"Right."

"So what happened to the same objects that you gave away?"

It was a metaphysical question that I'd avoided answering for myself.

Kathy grabbed her brown leather purse from her side, set it on her lap, and opened it up.

"I don't know. I guess they must have just disappeared. Because they weren't real."

"Then how do you explain this?" Kathy removed the wooden egg from her purse and held it up like some corny TV detective revealing the one piece of evidence needed for a conviction. "I'd like to believe you, David, but even in the realm of miracles, it doesn't make any sense." She slumped against the wall and quietly set the egg down beside her. She had rested her case and her silence indicated a verdict: *guilty by reason of insanity*.

I thought back on the moment when I dumped the bag and its contents out into the snow and then realized: "It wasn't there."

"What?

"When I poured out all the stuff, the egg wasn't there. It wasn't with the other things."

"How convenient. Come on. Where did the egg really come from—an antique store? Something you bought on eBay?"

"I remember when Sheena and I found the carpetbag in the field . . . the egg was already there inside the bag. It was among the women's clothes. So was the cameo brooch and the music box and the train tickets."

"What are you talking about?"

I continued to think out loud. "Elizabeth was wearing the cameo when Maggie and I met her in the bedroom."

"And who exactly is Elizabeth again?"

"She was the elderly lady that I proposed to."

"You asked a woman to marry you?"

I had left that part out when initially relating the story. "Yeah, she was about eighty. But it's okay. She wasn't real. She was like a ghost or an angel or something."

"How can that be, since you don't believe in angels?"

"Apparently they can be very convincing when they want to be."

"This may be a moot point, but why did you propose to this woman?"

"Well, when a Cracker Jack ring came out of the bag — it was a gift for Elizabeth — Maggie thought it was a sign of some sort that meant I was supposed to ask the old woman to marry me." I could see I was losing Kathy, understandably so.

"And this Elizabeth lady, you didn't tell her that you were already married?"

"No, because it wasn't me. You see, Elizabeth thought I was this guy named James, and she apologized for having — "

"What? Who?" Kathy looked very confused.

"James. She thought I was her boyfriend named James."

"You started to say she apologized for something — what?"

"She said that she had been having second thoughts about our love. Pretty weird, huh."

Kathy looked off to the side. "Very weird. In this little fantasy of yours, did this James character happen to have a last name?"

"Emerson. James Emerson."

Kathy looked like she was going to cry. I assumed they were tears of sympathy brought on by the mental breakdown of her estranged husband.

She rummaged through her purse. I thought she was searching for a Kleenex, but instead she pulled out a small white envelope, the edges of which were discolored with age.

"What's that?" I asked.

"I was over at my mom's house today. We were in her attic going through a trunk full of my grandma's old stuff when we came across this."

Kathy slipped a card out of the envelope and handed it to me. Watercolor violets on the front were rich and vibrant in color but smelled musty. I opened up the card. On the right hand side was an elegantly handwritten note in sepia ink.

> *Dear James,*
> *Thank you for the beautiful gift. Your generosity makes it all the more difficult to express my regret that I fear our future together is not to be. Enclosed you will find your heart. Please keep it safe until it's time to share it with someone more deserving than I.*
>
> *Sincerely,*
> *Elizabeth*

I looked up at Kathy. "It's just a coincidence, right—the names?"

Kathy handed me the envelope. Above the address, written in beautiful calligraphy, was the name *James Emerson*.

"My grandmother was eighteen when she wrote that letter to her boyfriend, James." Kathy said. "How do you explain this?"

How could I? The gift shop closet had suddenly blown open,

bringing Elizabeth back to life for a moment. "I can't," I finally said. "Your grandmother never married James?"

"Actually she did. When my mother found the letter it was still sealed."

I looked at the front of the envelope. In the top, right-hand corner was an un-cancelled, red two-cent stamp with George Washington's portrait.

"My grandmother never mailed it. She obviously had a change of heart and decided to give their relationship another chance. They had six kids and eight grandchildren before they died in a train accident."

"What?" This was more than just a coincidence. This was the world spinning around with Kathy's fate and mine in mind since the day that Sheena and I found the carpetbag in the field.

"What was that business in the letter about returning James's heart?" I asked.

Kathy nodded in the direction of the envelope in my hand. I opened it up and removed a thin, one-inch long wooden heart, the red paint half chipped off.

"I've been afraid to check something," Kathy said. She picked up the egg and twisted off layer after layer of shell until she came to the solid inner egg. She twisted it open, revealing the concave heart impression. She held it face up in front of me. I set the wooden heart-shaped piece into the impression . . . and it fit. A perfect fit.

Kathy looked up at me. She bit her top lip as tears began sliding down her cheeks. "Maybe there's a reason for the gift you gave me after all." She leaned forward and hugged me.

I hadn't held her in months, and now I wasn't eager to let go. That space between us, the feeling of being removed from the moment, that view from the cheap seats, was gone—replaced by an intimacy both familiar and new to me. Elizabeth was right. Hearts were bewildering things.

Kathy leaned back. She took hold of my hands, just as she had four days ago in her living room when she told me our relationship had suffered its final blow.

"Look, I don't know if things can ever work out between us again," she said, "but like Elizabeth . . . I'd like to give it one more try."

Of all the miracles I'd experienced over the past few days, those words topped the list. I'd been given the do-over of my life. "Thank you. I love you so much, Kathy. . . ."

"I love you, too, David."

I detected a reservation in her voice.

"But you need to know there's another gap, a bigger gap that needs to be bridged," she said. "And it's not between you and me, or you and the kids."

I knew where she was going with this, but for the first time, I paid attention.

"This journey," she continued, "this incredible journey that you went on . . . I'm so glad it's brought you closer to your family, but I don't think it was just about that. God forgave you for the biggest mistake you ever made in your life. But you can be forgiven for *every* mistake in your life. And this journey you were on . . . the change it made in your heart will pale in comparison to the changes your heart will undergo when you give your life up to him."

"You always tell me how you're being molded into the person that God wants you to be, that you're a work in progress."

"Yes?"

"So am I."

Kathy understood and hugged me again. "Listen," she said, "I'm sure the kids would love to know that you're here."

"You think I have time to see them?"

"If you hurry."

I took Kathy's hand, and together we stepped out of the baptistery. To our left in the dimly lit backstage area, a hyperactive kid in a sheep costume was bouncing off the other animals, much to their dismay. A young woman teacher wielding a bright flashlight called out to the crazed sheep, "Get over here, Frankie."

"Kelly's over there," Kathy said to me, pointing in the direction of the group of animals. "I'll save a seat for you." She squeezed my hand and kissed me gently on the lips before turning and walking down the stairs.

I entered the congested backstage area, wondering if Kelly, too, would be mad at me for my disappearing act. Since she was the only cow, it was easy to pick her out of the crowd.

"Kelly," I called out. She turned toward me and let loose with a wonderful, wide-eyed, open-mouthed look of joy.

"Daddy!" She made a beeline for my open arms. I knelt down and she wrapped her furry hooves around my neck and kissed me on the cheek. "You came," she said in a surprised and pleased little voice.

I felt my heart melt—a cliché that I'd heard all my life but never understood until that moment.

"How do I look?" Kelly asked, grabbing her long tail and spinning around, showing off her brown and white spotted cow costume.

I composed myself. "You make a cute cow." I poked at her black nose. "I'll bet you'd make a cute hamburger too. Good enough to eat." I took a fake bite out of her neck, tickling her and making her giggle wildly. That laugh alone made up for all the time I'd spent away from her. I propped my knee up and Kelly sat down on my leg.

"Are you ready to go on?"

Kelly became very serious. "I'm a little scared."

"That's okay," I said. "Everybody is scared before they go out on stage, but once you get out there, you'll be fine."

Kelly stared at me, then blurted out, "Moo, moo, moo."

"Very good," I said. "That's the best cow impersonation I've ever heard."

"Do you know what that means in cow talk?"

"No, what does that mean in cow talk?" I asked.

"It means 'I love you, Daddy.'"

More meltage. I pulled her in toward me and kissed her forehead. My throat began to close down around the words, but I got them out in the knick of time. "I love you, too, Kelly."

"All animals over here right now," Kelly's teacher announced, rescuing me from a complete meltdown.

"I gotta go, Daddy."

"Have fun, Kell."

She smiled and ran over to her teacher's side.

A hand on my arm helped me to my feet. I turned toward Pastor Neal.

"David, I may need your help."

"What do you mean? What for?"

He motioned for me to follow him. He led me across the dark stage, through the hay scattered in front of the nativity scene, and over to a small, center stage set consisting of a simple wooden table and chairs. A little girl wearing a plain white cotton dress and sash was holding a broom and nervously pacing nearby. Her black hair was tucked inside her shawl.

"Hey, Dad," Jeremy softly shouted.

I stopped, looked up to my right, and there, upstage on a black, fifteen-foot high platform, dangling his feet over the edge, sat my son. Dressed in a white outfit with his angel wings spread out behind him, he waved down to me.

The sight was terrifying. I flashed back to Ethan on the roof and Sheena on the limb. "I had no idea he was going to be up so high. Are you sure it's safe?"

"He's fine."

A barely visible cable extended up from Jeremy's back, disappearing into the darkness above him. I tried to contain my anxiety. I gave him a confident wave, hoping he was in good hands.

"David, over here," Neal said, a controlled panic in his voice. He led me over to the side of the stage and behind a translucent black nylon flat. There, slouched in a folding chair, was Terry, his face and hair drenched in sweat. He was massaging his flannel-shirted belly. Alongside him a cable hung from a pulley that was attached to a beam high above.

"You feeling any better?" Neal asked Terry.

"I think I'll be okay," Terry said, and immediately began gagging. Covering his mouth, he stood up, dashed across the stage in front of a wide-eyed Jeremy, and off the other side.

Pastor Neal turned toward me. "We suspect a tuna salad sandwich. If your son's going to fly tonight, he's going to need your help."

"My help? Wait a minute. You aren't suggesting—"

"Is everything okay?" Jeremy called.

"Everything's fine. Your dad's going to help out."

"No, no, I can't do this," I said.

The mini-orchestra began playing "Angels We Have Heard on High."

Neal picked up a pair of workman's gloves off the chair. "The first thing you need to do is put these on."

"Oh, come on, there must be someone else who can do this," I said. "Maybe Terry will be back. He didn't look all that sick to me."

Neal tossed the gloves in my direction. "All you need to do is hold on tight to the cable like this." He grabbed onto the cable, one hand above the other.

"You know, you look like you know what you're doing there. How 'bout if you work the cable, Pastor?"

"Sorry. Can't. Bad back."

"Well, maybe Gabriel could, you know, just walk into Mary's house."

"He's not a door-to-door salesman, David. He's an angel, arriving to deliver news that will change the world forever. It's only proper that he make a grand entrance."

"Please don't put this in my hands, Pastor."

"Now the moment before Jeremy steps off the platform, pull down on the cable," he said.

"But I don't even know when that happens."

"I'll give you the cue. And once the lights hit him, you'll be able to see him from here. Don't worry. The harness will carry him forward on the stage. Just try not to take too long easing him down, or he'll start swinging back and forth. And don't let him down too fast, or he may fall on his face when he lands on the stage. Other than that, you've got nothing to worry about."

"I don't know about this, Neal. I need more time to think

about it. Maybe we could rehearse it. When does this take place in the play?"

Through the stage curtains I could see the houselights dim.

"Right now."

"What?" I never realized how much moisture was lurking beneath my palms, waiting for a moment just like this to spring forth. "I can't do it."

Neal grabbed me firmly by the shoulders, looked me straight in the eyes. and with surprising intensity said, "Of course you can. Your son is counting on you, David. You are going to do this, and it's going to be fine."

He broke away from me and marched over to the side of the flat and looked around the corner at Jeremy.

I quickly stuffed my hands in the gloves and grabbed onto the cable. As I stood holding onto his lifeline, I realized Jeremy *was* counting on me. I wondered, as he prepared to take that leap of faith off the platform, if he were considering all the times in the past when his father had let him down.

Two little kids ran out to center stage and grabbed onto the backside of the curtain, which was divided down the middle. They ran back in opposite directions, holding onto the curtain, opening it to the audience. From my vantage point I could see a soft spotlight come up on the girl standing downstage, sweeping the straw floor with the broom. The rest of the stage remained in darkness.

The music faded and was replaced by a James Earl Jones sound-alike . . .

"In the days of Herod 'the angel Gabriel was sent from God to a city of Galilee named Nazareth, to a virgin betrothed to a man whose name was Joseph, of the house of David; and the virgin's name was Mary.'"

I readjusted my hands up higher on the cable, tightening my grip.

A second spotlight, this one midnight blue, shone on Jeremy as he stood high above the stage, his wings spread out majestically.

My heart was about to exit my chest like that creature in *Alien* as I pulled the rope taut. I felt both proud and panicked at the same time. In the darkness the platform seemed to disappear beneath Jeremy, giving him the appearance of floating in midair.

I was a wreck. I needed help. *Please, God, don't let me mess this up*, raced through my mind.

Neal raised his arm, looked over at me, and thrust a pointed finger in my direction. I pulled the weight of my body up on the cable. Jeremy stepped off the platform—and was airborne.

I'm not sure what happened next, or how it happened. I don't remember sliding my hands down the cable or using a hand-over-fist method to lower Jeremy. All I know is that my son, bathed in the blue spotlight, flew down as gracefully as any angel possibly could have. His wings spread out wide as his arms reached out forward, his palms turned up. He stepped down onto the stage in front of the girl playing Mary as effortlessly as if those wings were actually his.

The audience burst into spontaneous applause. Pastor Neal looked over at me with one of his big smiles and a thumbs-up gesture.

On stage Mary backed away from the angel Gabriel, dropped her broom, and fell to her knees.

Jeremy's voice, strong and confident, declared, "Hail, O favored one, the Lord is with you!"

Mary crouched behind the table out of fear.

I couldn't have been prouder of Jeremy.

"Do not be afraid, Mary, for you have found favor with God. And behold, you will conceive in your womb and bear a son, and you shall call his name Jesus."

As I watched the little Mary come out of hiding, Pastor Neal walked over to me and shook my hand. I was sure he was about to say how wonderfully I had come through and how thankful he was, but instead he simply said, "See, you didn't mess up! Praise be to God!"

Terry, still looking considerably peaked, shuffled up and joined us as we watched Gabriel finish explaining to Mary her role in the salvation story. The stage lights dimmed, then went out completely, ending the scene. Jeremy unhooked the cable from his back and rushed off stage, meeting Neal alongside of the flat.

"You did great, Jeremy, just great," Neal said, playfully mussing up the hair on the top of his head.

"Thanks." Jeremy looked over at me as I took off the gloves. I held out my arms, and he walked into them and buried his face in my chest. His body heaved a couple times as if he might be crying. I wrapped him up in my arms, not knowing exactly where the emotions were coming from.

"Nice job, kiddo. You were terrific."

Kathy was probably wondering if I'd left town again, so I figured I'd better get back to rejoin her. I exited the backstage door, which led outside, and began to walk back around to the front of the church in order to not disturb the performance. I was feeling pretty good about myself, heroic, even—I had shown up at the last second and saved the day.

I flashed my ticket stub to a woman at the door and slipped into the dark sanctuary, behind the last row of seats, eager to tell

Kathy how I had performed in the clutch.

Several little shepherds and sheep wandered around the stage while the orchestra performed "Silent Night." As I began my walk down the center aisle toward the front, I noticed a young man in a suit step out into the aisle from one of the front pews. Walking in my direction, he kept his eyes on the carpet in front of him. He must not have seen me because, as he began to pass me, we bumped shoulders. He stopped just for a moment and looked at me. It was the strangest sensation. I didn't recognize him, but his presence felt familiar, like I should have known him.

"Sorry," he whispered.

"No problem," I said.

Had that been the end of the exchange, I don't suppose I would have thought a whole lot more about it. But before turning away, under his breath he said, "Ain't easy to fly without help."

At first I thought, *What a strange thing to say. What exactly did he mean? Did he know that Jeremy was my son, or that I had helped him?* I tried to let it go as I sat down next to Kathy in the aisle seat she had saved for me.

"I thought we'd lost you again," she said.

Then I remembered where I'd heard the man's words before. I turned around and craned my neck into the aisle. I could just barely make him out in the darkness as he stopped at the end of the aisle, turned around, looked all the way back down at me. And then he did something that made every hair on the back of my neck stand at attention: He gave me the Cub Scout salute, then smiled and walked out of the sanctuary. John Newton had fulfilled his promise.

"David?" Kathy tried to get my attention. I turned back around toward her. "Is everything all right?"

"Yeah. It's fine."

"Did you see Jeremy's entrance?"

"Yeah, I did," I said.

"It was unbelievable, wasn't it?"

"Miraculous."

etc.

bonus content includes:

READER'S GUIDE

1. God frequently uses angels to deliver his messages to mortals, and, in fact, Scripture tells us that his angels specifically watch over and guide us: "For He shall give His angels charge over you, to keep you in all your ways" (Psalm 91:11, NKJV); "Are not all angels ministering spirits sent to serve those who will inherit salvation?" (Hebrews 1:14, NIV). Discuss which characters might have been angels and the message they brought to David.

2. Have you ever suspected that you may have encountered an angel? What happened? What was the message conveyed?

3. As the story begins, we soon understand David's dilemma, his sense of alienation from people—and specifically from his wife—yet he opens up to a stranger, Maggie. Why is he able to do this? When Maggie first meets David, she is in a very vulnerable state, yet she, too, opens up and trusts David. Why do you think this is?

4. The relationship between David and the bag is a unique one. Talk about the stages and changes in their relationship as the journey progresses. How does Maggie's relationship with the bag and the faith she begins to develop in it contribute to David's redemption?

5. Consider the following passage:

> Our marriage counselor had suggested more than
> once that I drank out of fear — to avoid my feelings.
> She'd frequently point her bony finger in my
> direction and say, "You, sir, need to get in touch with
> your feelings" — like it was just a matter of picking
> up the phone and calling Aunt Louise or something.
> The fact was "Aunt Louise" had been buried long
> ago, having died of some undisclosed disease.

   What is David actually hinting at?

6. Part of David's transformation occurs through the gesture
   of giving these gifts to strangers. Offer examples of
   particular gifts that materialize in the bag and how they
   move David to act in a compassionate way.
7. The personification of the carpetbag turns it into an
   important "character" in the story. Describe some of
   its personality traits, at which moments these traits are
   revealed, and how they influence David's relationship
   with the bag and his disconnection from people.
8. *The Reluctant Journey of David Connors* makes frequent
   use of heart imagery. For example, the gift that David
   gives Kathy is a wooden egg with the impression of
   a heart inside. How does this gift represent his own
   heart condition, and in what way does it symbolically
   bookend his journey? When Elizabeth says, "Hearts are
   bewildering things, aren't they? They can be soft, pliable,
   innocent, open wide to all the possibilities that love has to

offer . . . or they can become hardened from experience. And the difference might be but a single beat." What might she be referring to?

9. When Maggie places her head on David's shoulder on the train, he says that the moment "filled me with an unfamiliar feeling—a tranquility that had escaped me for the longest time." In what other ways does Maggie's presence on the journey change David?

10. David said he finally had to stop attending church with Kathy because he realized that when heads bowed for prayer, his mind wandered in order to avoid a confrontation with the God he still resented for having taken his mom. In what ways does that conflict become resolved?

11. How does David's journey parallel a Christian/spiritual journey? Which parts of the story reflect man's search for God? Which mirror man's fears in that search? His joys? His difficulties in accepting love and forgiveness unmerited? What do you believe to be David's most difficult task on his journey?

12. The death of David's mom was obviously a traumatic event for him. How did her passing affect his life? What were some of David's attitudes toward his mom and the role she played in his life, and how—at the end of David's journey—did those attitudes change?

13. Early on, David informs Pastor Neal that he's "doing just fine these days believing in only what these eyes of mine can see." Give examples of how the carpetbag forces him to have faith in more than what's visible.

14. Both David and Maggie are dramatically affected by events from their past. Are there any events from your

childhood, big or small, for which you've carried guilt or regret into your adult life or which have crippled the way you currently relate to people or to God? Who was your first childhood friend, and how did he or she influence your life? Do you still own any objects from your childhood? What significance do they hold for you?

15. At the end of the story David unearths the actual carpetbag that he buried in his childhood, and he dumps the contents onto the ground. Each real-life trinket had a counterpart that played a part in David's journey of self-discovery. Or did it? Was every item accounted for?

16. Just before David chooses to let Ethan look inside the carpetbag, and when he spots Ethan catching snowflakes on his tongue, he sees something familiar in the boy. What he sees is himself. In what ways is Ethan symbolic of David's inner, spiritual struggle? When David encounters Ethan trapped on the chapel roof, how does that struggle play out?

17. Flight plays an important metaphoric role in the story: Ethan's obsession with airplanes, the feather that came out of the bag, the balsa glider toy, David's own childhood memories of flight, the bottle rocket, and Jeremy's role as the angel Gabriel. In what ways does this imagery represent freedom, specifically as it applies to David?

18. In what ways is John Newton's comment about flight prophetic?

19. When David returns from his odyssey, what are some indications that he may have begun to change?

20. Self-awareness and forgiveness are two themes in the book. In what ways did David's repression of memories benefit

him, and in what ways did this defense mechanism betray him? Why do you believe it was so difficult for him to accept forgiveness?

CARPETBAG TRIVIA

CARPETBAG

As the number of railroads multiplied in the 1840s and 1850s, subsequently multiplying the number of common travelers, there arose an immediate need to manufacture inexpensive luggage. The 1860s were the heyday of the carpetbag, a piece of luggage that, as its name suggests, is made from a remnant of carpet, usually oriental in design. Durable and rugged, the carpetbag could be purchased at one's local dry goods store for one to two dollars.[1]

FEATHER

In general, birds carry one third of their feathers on their head. The total number of feathers varies widely from bird to bird, from the Ruby Hummingbird, which has only 940 feathers, to the Whistling Swan, which, in winter, can have as many as 25,000 feathers on its body. So, too, can the length of feathers vary, from the most minute down to the stunningly long (the record is 34.75 feet) tail feathers of a Japanese breed of ornamental chicken.[2]

CAMEO BROOCH

During Queen Victoria's reign in the 1840s, women's clothing became very confining, covering up the wrist, the neck, and even the ears. For this reason brooches became the obvious jewelry of choice. A valued souvenir for a Victorian woman was a cameo with her likeness carved in relief into lava rock or stone by an Italian artist. While commissioned portraits were still expensive, the industrialization of the eighteenth and nineteenth centuries made possible the mass production of cameo brooches, featuring still attractive, but now more anonymous women's faces.[3]

BABE RUTH AUTOGRAPHED BASEBALL

His larger-than-life persona coupled with his incredible talents on the baseball field made Babe Ruth the highest-paid baseball player of his era—$80,000 in 1930. When informed that his salary was $5,000 more than President Hoover's, Ruth responded, "I had a better year than he did."[4] Today, depending on its condition, a baseball autographed by the Babe can be worth between $1,500 and $20,000.[5]

GREEN EGGS AND HAM

Rumor has it that Dr. Seuss's publisher, Bennett Cerf (a regular panelist on the game show *What's My Line?* from 1951 to 1967), bet the good doctor $50 that he couldn't write a book using only fifty words, and the resulting effort was *Green Eggs and Ham*. The silly rhyming tale is written in the cumulative story tradition used in English folklore. Published in 1962, *Green Eggs and Ham* has gone on to be the fourth-best-selling children's book of all time, having sold more than seven million copies as of 2004.[6]

The Box Camera

In 1888, George Eastman introduced the box camera, just four years after introducing flexible celluloid film. This was the first camera available to the general public. Equipped with a fixed-focus lens and a single shutter speed, it could be purchased for $25.[7]

Sunglasses

Sunglasses as we now know them were first used in China in the twelfth century or earlier. The eyes were protected from the sun's rays by two flat panes of smoky quartz.[8] With the advent of plastics, the sunglasses business experienced a boom in the 1940s. It was the 1950s when the cat's eye style for women came into vogue.

Balsa Wood Glider

As a World War I U. S. Navy aviator, Paul K. Guillow's interest in flying led him to create and market a line of balsa wood construction kits of famous combat aircraft in 1926. With America's interest in Charles Lindbergh's solo flight across the Atlantic, the model plane business boomed until the Second World War's demand for balsa in the manufacturing of life jackets and rafts forced Guillow to use less successful paper cardboard and pine. Post-war prosperity and the new plastic models caused plummeting sales in the kit business, so Guillow turned his efforts toward producing inexpensive hand-launched and rubber band–powered gliders. In 1953, the *Jetfire* glider was introduced for 10 cents. It was the first glider to be mass-produced and packaged on a high-speed packaging machine, enabling Guillow to keep up with the booming economy by selling his gliders in the up-and-coming chain stores.[9]

RAGGEDY ANN AND ANDY DOLLS

Legend has it that Johnny Gruelle, artist and creator of the Raggedy Ann phenomenon, was rummaging around the attic as an adult when he came upon a doll that his mom had made for his sister years earlier. He found this doll to be great fodder for stories that he told his daughter, Marcella. In May of 1915, Gruelle filed for a patent application for the doll, and a month later, a trademark application for the logo "Raggedy Ann." It was only a few months later that his daughter became ill and died from complications after a vaccination. The first actual book, *Raggedy Ann's Stories*, was published in 1918 and was followed by dozens more, often marketed with the doll. Eighty-nine years later, the franchise is a heartfelt tribute to Marcella's memory.[10]

WOODEN NESTING EGG

The concept of nesting eggs—a set of eggs of decreasing sizes placed one inside another—appeared in 1885 when the first Fabergé egg was introduced. Very popular as Russian folk art, *matryoshka* dolls, painted in bright colors and varnished, were inspired by souvenir dolls from Japan. Many of these dolls are designed to follow a theme, such as fairy tales, pagan gods, peasant families, or political leaders.[11]

MUSIC BOX

In the fourteenth century a bell-ringer created the first mechanical music in the form of a cylinder with pins, which operated cams that then struck a series of bells. Not much was made of this oddity until Swiss brothers by the name of Jaquet-Droz, who were clockmakers, created a mechanical singing bird in 1780. In 1796, Antoine Favre, a clockmaker from Geneva, came up with the idea of replacing the bells with combs of pretuned metallic notes, producing a more precise melody. The first music boxes were produced in Sainte-Croix in 1811, surpassing the Swiss watch-making industry and representing 10 percent of Switzerland's export. In 1870, a German inventor developed a music box using discs—the precursor to the phonograph, which Thomas Edison invented in 1877. In 1892, German immigrant Gustave Brachhausen established the Regina Music Box Company in New Jersey, which sold more than 100,000 music boxes until the popularity of the phonograph and the falling economy forced its closure in 1921.[12]

CRACKER JACK RING

While selling popcorn from a cart in Chicago in the 1870s, German immigrant Frederick William Rueckheim, along with his brother, Louis, came up with the popcorn candy known as Cracker Jack. They introduced their mass-produced product at the Chicago World's Fair in 1893, but it wasn't until 1912 that they packaged toy surprises in every box. In 1986, it was estimated that over 17 billion toys had been placed inside Cracker Jack boxes. The trademark logos of Sailor Jack and his dog, Bingo, were introduced in 1919 and were modeled after Frederick's grandson, Robert, and his dog.[13]

1. The Carpetbagger, "Brief History of Carpetbags and Carpetbaggers," http://www.thecarpetbagger.com/history.html.
2. Gordon Ramel, "The Wonder of Bird Feathers," Earth-Life, http://www.earthlife.net/birds/feathers.html.
3. Monica Lynn Clements, "Victorian Cameos," *New England Antiques Journal*, http://www.antiquesjournal.com/Pages04/archives/cameos.html.

4. The Idea Logical Company, "Babe Ruth," Baseball Library.com, http://www.baseballlibrary.com/ballplayers/player.php?name=Babe_Ruth_1895

5. Answers.com, "Babe Ruth Autographed Baseballs," WikiAnswers, http://www.faqfarm.com/Q/What_is_the_value_of_an_autographed_Babe_Ruth_baseball.

6. The Wikimedia Foundation, Inc. "Green Eggs and Ham," Wikipedia, http://en.wikipedia.org/wiki/Green_Eggs_and_Ham.

7. Photography.com, "History of Cameras and Photography," http://www.photography.com/history-of-photography.php.

8. The Wikimedia Foundation, Inc. "Sunglasses," Wikipedia, http://en.wikipedia.org/wiki/Glasses#Sunglasses.

9. Paul K. Guillow, Inc., "History of Paul K. Guillow, Inc." Guillow.com, http://guillow.com/GuillowInfo.asp?UID=2896384.

10. Barbara Crews, "Raggedy Ann and Andy Dolls," About, http://collectibles.about.com/od/raggedyann/a/aa032099.htm.

11. The Wikimedia Foundation, Inc. "Matryoshka Dolls," http://en.wikipedia.org/wiki/Matryoshka_doll.

12. The Wikimedia Foundation, Inc. "Musical Box," http://en.wikipedia.org/wiki/Music_box.

13. Mary Bellis, "Cracker Jack," About, http://inventors.about.com/library/inventors/blcrackerjacks.htm.

ACKNOWLEDGMENTS

I want to thank Len Hill for his years of dedication and support, as well as Will Shetterly and Emma Bull for their insightful workshop. Thanks to Jill Grosjean for her belief and perseverance; to Jamie Chavez and Reagen Reed for their deft editing; to Jeff Gerke, Kris Wallen, and the NavPress team for their hard work. A special thanks to Dustye Nader, Denise Soulam, Rick Locke, Marilyn Kaddatz, and Adryan Russ for their helpful critiques, to Jay Miller, Frank DeMore, and others for their crucial words of encouragement along the way; and to Morgan and Graham for their light in my life. Thank you to Susan for her love and unenviable job of bolstering a fragile confidence. And finally, I give my eternal gratitude to the One who has always loved D. C. and me, even when the feelings weren't mutual.

ABOUT THE AUTHOR

DON LOCKE graduated from Southern Illinois University in 1971 with a BS in radio/TV and minors in film and fine arts. Over the years he's managed to mix these interests, working as a fine artist, TV writer, playwright, and freelance illustrator for books, magazines, and television. He has worked as a graphic artist/illustrator for *The Tonight Show* for the past twenty-seven years. Don lives in Glendale, California, with his wife, Susan. He has two grown sons, Morgan and Graham. *The Reluctant Journey of David Connors* is his first novel.

CHECK OUT THESE OTHER GREAT TITLES FROM THE NAVPRESS FICTION LINE!

Around the World in 80 Dates
Christa Ann Banister

ISBN-13: 978-1-60006-177-6
ISBN-10: 1-60006-177-X

Travel writer Sydney Alexander is ready for one particular journey to end: her frustrating search for a Mr. Right. But things are looking way up. Just after landing her dream job, she meets an eligible round of bachelors. Now Sydney will discover just how far she's willing to compromise to land her dream guy.

The Restorer
Sharon Hinck

ISBN-13: 978-1-60006-131-8
ISBN-10: 1-60006-131-1

Meet Susan, a housewife and soccer mom whose dreams stretch far beyond her ordinary world. While studying the book of Judges, Susan longs to be a modern-day Deborah. She gets her wish for adventure when she stumbles through a portal into an alternate universe and encounters a nation locked in a fierce struggle for survival.

The Restorer's Son
Sharon Hinck

ISBN-13: 978-1-60006-132-5
ISBN-10: 1-60006-132-X

After the battle of Morsal Plains, Susan Mitchell returned to her world looking forward to a little normalcy. What she found sent her and her husband, Mark, rushing back through the portal to the gray world of Lyric and Hazor, desperately searching for their missing son. Assassins, political intrigue, and false leads beset their path, which takes them into the darkness of Hazor on the heels of the new Restorer, who is on the run from his calling.

To order copies, visit your local Christian bookstore, call NavPress at
1-800-366-7788, or log on to www.navpress.com.
To locate a Christian bookstore near you, call 1-800-991-7747.